I0748912

Sunset over Chania

By Annette Creswell

Outer Banks Publishing Group
Raleigh/Outer Banks

 Published in the United States of America by Outer Banks Publishing Group – Outer Banks/Raleigh.

www.outerbankspublishing.com

For information contact Outer Banks Publishing Group at

info@outerbankspublishing.com

Cover photos by Brett Creswell

FIRST EDITION – August 2024
Library of Congress Control Number: 2024942331
ISBN – 979-8-9907093-4-8
eISBN – 979-8-9907093-5-5

Also by Annette Creswell

79 UXBRIDGE ROAD

Tom, who was previously an Accountant in the shipping office of Cunard, has arrived home from the second world war to his wife Martha and their two children, Brian who is five and Janey eleven.

Because of the terrible conditions in the concentration camp in which he was imprisoned by the Germans, Tom contracts TB and is subsequently admitted to a sanitarium leaving Martha to care for the family.

Tom's mother who lives in style in Belgravia does not endear herself to anyone and blames her son's ill health on his enlistment in the war. However, Martha's mother is the complete opposite to Grandma Johnson, and Brian and Janey adore visiting her in the school holidays.

In Martha's struggle to care for her family, she is supported by her gossipy but kind neighbour, Ethel, who lives next door and likes to play Bingo at the local hall.

Tom dies of TB, but he did not die alone as Edward, the kind doctor at the sanitarium had been with him in his final moments.

Will Martha be able to support herself and her two children with no husband? Will she find love again when everything looks so hopeless?

The Lodgers

When Mabel, a former Vaudeville performer, lands a job managing a boarding house on the ocean, she appears to attract a disparate cast of lodgers, all with unfortunate and dark lives.

The lodgers include:

Two queens, old thespian friends of Mabel's who live in the basement with a peppercorn rent.

Therese is a pregnant Irish girl banished to England by her mother who assumes she is in an unmarried mother's home in the care of the nuns.

Irene, a recovering alcoholic who has a sister

Judy, due to a trauma experienced during the war is unable to speak.

Arthur, an aged army major, had a son Ned who was shot for desertion.

Harry, alias Percy, a con man and felon who befriends the landlady,

Mabel. When Therese moves to the Outback to get married, Judy follows and one day Judy spots a Kookaburra in a nearby tree. When the bird laughs, an unexpected, wondrous miracle happens.

The Dark Before the Dawn

Just before the start of World War II, Peggy Davis, a London midwife, has a chance encounter with a stranger that changes her life forever.

When Peggy meets Charles, a wealthy lord as she boards a bus in front of Harrods department store, fate casts them together.

When Charles' wife, Diana, and first child die in childbirth, Peggy, and Charles are thrust into a relationship of happiness, sorrow, and unexpected tragedy.

They ultimately marry, have a son, and adopt an east-end refugee boy from London.

What transpires is a web of family dramas a la Downton Abbey with lesbian relationships, Nazi sympathizers, and family secrets revealed as Peggy attempts to navigate through her new life from midwife to lady of the manor.

Life's Last Page

Into the confines of Waverley Nursing Home steps Lisa, a voluntary worker whose life has been scarred by emotional and physical abuse. Firstly, by her mother then by her Attorney husband, Gary.

Tormented by her own painful past, she becomes a guardian angel for the suffering residents, particularly Harry whose own life had been one of hardship and suffering.

Olga, a survivor of the Holocaust, was another resident Lisa befriends and to them she offers solace in the most controversial way possible.

Into the picture comes Douglas, a flawed character who harbours a deep secret which leads him down a treacherous path. Haunted by his own demons he too seeks an elusive redemption that seems forever out of reach.

As these two complex souls collide, their actions ignite a series of events that will test the boundaries of morality. In a world where right and wrong blur into shades of grey, will they find absolution or be forever consumed by their own darkness?

Chapter One

She trod warily over the cobblestones holding on to her son as they passed the vine draped alfresco cafes and tiny shops which heightened her sense of rapture. They pushed on down and down towards the harbour to the restaurants with their menus displayed in Greek and English. The irascible ocean thrust waves onto the promenade swamping tourists who were unaware of this normal occurrence here in beautiful Chania.

They walked along scanning the menus.

"What about we go here?" said Meg. "They have calamari and it's right at the edge of the harbour."

"Ok, yes, great," replied Theo.

"Yassou," greeted the waiter as he escorted them to a table far away from where she wanted to sit.

"Oh, please can we sit at that one?" Meg pleaded pointing to a table at the edge nearest the ocean.

"Surely, if you don't mind getting a little wet."

"No, we won't mind at all, will we Theo?"

Her son nodded in agreement albeit a little uncertain.

The waiter seated them at the requested table and flourished a menu.

"I think I will have a glass of Prosecco. Are you going to have a beer?"

"You know too much about me mother," Theo replied. "There's nothing like a cold beer when it's this hot."

The weather had been stifling since they arrived in Crete. Last night the temperature had been 39 degrees at 7.00pm. Theo had been concerned that his mother would not cope. Although still sprightly, she had just celebrated her 90th birthday in the Intercontinental Plus Grand hotel in Paris. That had been her gift from him a luxurious night in the most sumptuous surrounds. Theo had even organised an upgrade which had turned out to be a presidential suite with no less than three balconies overlooking the streets of Paris. Meg had been astounded when the taxi had pulled up at the grand entrance a liveried porter dealing with their bags.

"What are we doing here?" Meg had asked completely confused as a booking had been made for another hotel which had been four stars not like this palace which would have rated ten!

"It's your birthday surprise mum," replied Theo as he took her arm escorting her through the marbled foyer festooned with huge vases of flowers and statuary. After they had investigated every corner of the suite and Theo had thrown open the windows so they could look down at the people walking along the street they had repaired to Les

Deux Magots for aperitifs and beef carpaccio. Theo managed to obtain a table at the edge of the footpath where they could witness the passing Parisian parade. Meg's wish had always been to experience this café famous for all the erstwhile authors and poets who frequented there: Hemingway, Picasso, Simone de Beauvoir to name a few. Dinner had been consumed across the road at another authors' haunt, Brasserie Lipp. Meg's delight had known no bounds as their night progressed but there had been one more surprise in store for them when they returned to the hotel. Awaiting on the coffee table in the sitting room was a bottle of champagne, a basket of strawberries, a gateau and a tin of biscuits. This was the cause of great amusement for mother and son, Meg remarking that the staff must have thought they were dealing with honeymooners or Theo was Meg's toy boy!

The waiter took their order and left them to peruse the menu.

"How about the calamari and the fried sardines?" Theo asked.

Meg was unsure about the sardines which had bony spines which she disliked but she knew Theo liked them so agreed. She could always split them with the knife and extricate the bones.

The waiter returned with their drinks.

"Can we have the calamari with lots of lemon and also the sardines?" asked Theo.

"Certainly," replied the waiter as he bustled off darting between the tightly packed tables filled with the ubiquitous tourists and a sprinkling of voluble locals.

Another wave washed over the promenade and under their table but, in anticipation, Meg had her feet tucked out of the way resting on the rung of the other chair. Theo however was taken unawares his attention diverted to the lighthouse being pummelled by the foam and fury of the waves.

"Bloody hell!" He expostulated.

"Don't worry, Theo it's only water and you're wearing sandals."

"I guess you're right."

They clinked their glasses.

"Cheers," they said as the waiter placed their order on the table.

Theo squeezed a lemon over the food as a skinny cat wandered past their table. Meg threw it a sardine which the cat sniffed rubbing its whiskers against it before taking a nibble.

"I think it's blind mum," offered Theo as the cat slunk off the sardine swept away by another wash of seawater.

"Poor thing," said Meg who was a cat person and owned a tabby presently being cared for by her neighbour.

By now, Theo had followed his mother's example and had his feet tucked away on the rung of the other chair and was now enjoying this unique experience.

She sipped her wine delighting in the effervescence and cast her eyes towards the magnificent 16th century Venetian lighthouse, standing sentinel warning the ships of the perilous conditions of the rocky shore. That lighthouse, a wonder to behold especially silhouetted before the setting sun. It meant so much to see it again and she would be forever grateful to her son for bringing her back to this place which was replete with memories both bitter and sweet. She had not told him that this would be the end of her travels, her sojourns with him to foreign climes. The tentacles of cancer were quickly spreading and her time on this earth was ending. When a pain gripped her, she would put it down to an old age twinge so alleviating Theo's concern. She knew she would greatly miss all the wonderful moments she had shared with him, her darling Theo. All the sights they had seen, their love of food and wine and swimming in the sea. Her jaunts had been just what she had needed after those turbulent years of her marriage those times when her husband controlled her life to the point of cutting her off from her friends. His violent temper leaving her bruised and cowering in corners as his fists rained blows on her body. She had tried to protect Theo from witnessing the violence but knew he would have heard the raised voices and thuds filtering into his bedroom. Meg had opined her husband's violence was a result of his time spent as a British soldier during the war. So, she remained in the marriage forgiving his transgressions hoping it would always be the last time she would be abused. However, fate had intervened when a coronary occlusion had saved them both. Jim, the perpetrator had passed away in an ambulance en route to the hospital. Meg had felt guilt about her inability to shed any tears for this man whom she had coerced into marrying.

Theo looked at his mother entranced just as he was by the idyllic scene before them especially the lighthouse pounded by the sea and intuited how amazing it would be to view it in the setting sun.

He voiced this thought.

"I think tonight we should return for dinner when the sun sets. I will ask the fellow at the hotel for his recommendation, one which has the best food and view."

"Oh, Theo," she exclaimed. "That would be so wonderful if we could do that."

"But," she added, "I don't want you to spend too much. You have already given me more than I deserve."

"Nonsense, mum," said Theo taking a good slurp of his beer

and attacking another piece of calamari.

"What is the good of money if you don't spend it? Life's too short to skimp on things such as these, and you never know when it might be the last time we get to do them."

How prophetic were his words, Meg thought. It would be the last time she would be here so if Theo wanted to indulge her then so be it.

"Pardon me for listening in," announced a man at the next table.

"But I heard you were wanting a good restaurant to watch the sunset?"

"Oh, yes we were actually, can you recommend one?"

"You can't do better than the Pallas. It has great food and if you can get an outdoor table nearest the edge, you will have a perfect view of the lighthouse with the sun setting behind it."

"Oh," replied Theo. "Thanks so much for your help. I was going to ask the hotel. Is it near here?"

" Yes, it's just over there near the Fortress," he said pointing in the direction and then continued with his lunch.

"Oh, wasn't it nice of that man Theo? I hope it's not booked up for tonight. By the sound of it, it's probably popular."

"I will give them a call now," said Theo taking his mobile.

"Ok, good luck," she said hoping that they could secure a table.

She overheard him talking asking for a specific table and agreeing on 5.00pm.

"Ok, we're in. I booked us for five o'clock at an outdoor table. We can order a cocktail and relax before the sun sets."

"Oh, Theo," said Meg. "That's marvellous, thank you."

Meg looked over to the Fortress which had stood on the same spot since 1620 to protect Chania's harbour. How wonderful it would be she thought to have dinner there, to watch the Grecian sun set with the lighthouse silhouetted before it. To drink a Margarita and more than one glass of champagne even though it was contraindicated with her painkillers. But so what if she got a little tipsy, Theo would be there to ensure nothing happened to her and he would be ordering a taxi to take them safely back to their hotel. She would ensure she had a good nap after lunch so she could enjoy the night. She thought tonight she would tell him a little about her time spent here in the war as up to now she had not divulged much information. He only knew she had been a nurse in Crete and that was all. Her thoughts turned to the caves which she knew were too inaccessible for her to visit and would she really want to after all this time? Nothing good would come of it. It was better to keep those memories locked away in her heart where only she had access to them.

Theo's phone pinged.

"Is that a text?" asked Meg as she meticulously parted the flesh from a sardine exposing the backbone which she extricated.

"Yes, it's from Kev."

"How's he going?"

Kevin was Theo's partner. They had been together for three years and recently Theo had moved in with him sharing a flat in Pimlico, his lawyer's salary well able to afford the rent to which Theo contributed as a celebrant for marriages and funerals. It took Meg a while to process the fact that her son was gay, that she would not see him married or have the pleasure of minding grandchildren.

However, Kevin seemed a nice enough person much better than some of the fellows with whom Theo had fraternised in the past. There had been one Meg had disliked, him with the dreadlocks and pasty face. She felt he could not be trusted, averting his eyes, and mooching around her house like he was on the lookout for something to steal. She could not see what Theo saw in him and was glad that he terminated the friendship. She was pleased that society was becoming more tolerant towards gays. Not as in the days of Oscar Wilde when it was a criminal offence.

"He's snowed under," Theo replied placing his phone on the table.

"Is he still working on that defamation case?"

"Yes, it's going to trial next week."

"Does he think he will win?"

"He hopes so. He has briefed one of the leading QC's but, like all these cases, it could go either way."

"Well, give him my love the next time you contact him and tell him I said to make sure he goes to bed at a reasonable hour. He doesn't want a recurrence of that virus he had."

"Yes mother," said Theo smiling, thinking how typical it was of her caring about the welfare of his partner as though he was her son.

Theo paid the bill then, assisting Meg from the table, they made their way slowly up the alley from whence they came their only thoughts of the wonderful evening lying in wait for them.

Chapter Two

When war broke out in 1939, Meg was keen to play an active part in the war effort. She began her nursing training with the Red Cross serving at a First Aid Post in London. With the Italian invasion in 1940 and as a nod to her interest in Greece, she joined the Greek Red Cross completing her nursing training. She was posted to an ambulance train tending and transporting the wounded from the Albanian front. When the Germans invaded, she and other medical staff managed to board a yacht gaining passage to Crete. The journey was perilous as the yacht was bombed killing many crew members however Meg survived albeit marooned on Kimolos island. She prayed that she and other wounded men and nurses would be rescued which is what occurred as another vessel picked them up and transported them to Chania, a journey which would take ten days. A large tented field hospital was established containing 600 beds and although it had Red Cross markings it was bombed and machine gunned. The medical staff then decided to move the hospital to some caves situated along the rocky coast and, although conditions were primitive, the staff managed to erect cooking areas, stretcher beds and hurricane lamps. .It was in one of these caves that a relationship had formed between Meg and one of her Greek patients, Stavros. He had suffered an artillery wound to his leg which necessitated regular debridement, a painful process of cutting away the dead tissue and foreign matter.

"Ahh," he moaned as she concentrated on her task. She hated it as much as he but knew it had to be done to avoid infection.

"Sorry, Stav," she uttered. The name she had bequeathed to him and which he had begun to like rolling off her tongue in that lilting voice. He also liked her tender ministrations and her beautiful eyes which tended to crinkle while undertaking this most distasteful of jobs.

"There, all done for now," she said briskly applying a clean dressing and pleased that it was over until the next time.

"Now, try to sleep and I'll look in on you later." It took all her strength not to lean over and place her lips on his forehead but she could not be seen to be favouring one patient over another whatever her feelings were.

She arose and, taking the bowl of infected tissue and the hurricane lamp, made her way over to another patient whose stomach wounds meant he would not last the night.

As she completed her duties, another cacophonous sound rent the air and the occupants of the cave hospital knew it was another bomb landing in the harbour not far from them. She settled into her camp bed on the dirt floor where goats had walked and prayed that everyone would remain safe and the war would soon end. Her ears were attuned to the other sounds in the cave, sounds of wounded men moaning and grunting and she focussed her attention on the terminally ill patient near her. It was not long until she heard the ominous sound of his dying breath. She arose and crept over to him. She held his hand and offered a prayer as his spirit left his body ascending into eternity. He would be another soul consigned to the sea joining all the others who had not survived their wounds. She draped the makeshift sheet over his face then made her way back to bed where, thoroughly exhausted, she gave herself up to sleep.

The weeks went on as did the relentless bombing and she wondered if they all would eventually be found and captured by the Germans. She had prepared herself for that eventuality however, she would rather be killed outright by machine guns than be taken as a prisoner of war.

"It's not looking too bad now Stav," she told him peering at his wound after she removed the dressing. "I think you might be lucky."

A grin lit his face.

"Efharisto, thank you for good nurse."

"Oh, I didn't do much except maybe give you pain," she replied adding, "you must have good healing skin."

As those words left her lips there was a terrible commotion at the entrance to the cave. Four Germans barged in demanding to know what was occurring here. Meg and the other nurses ran towards each other their Red Cross insignia on their uniforms clearly visible. They were terrified of their fate and the fate of their patients. What would happen to all of them now?

Chapter Three

Fortune had favoured them that day as their lives had been spared. The nurses and some of the patients including Stavros had been sent to a hospital in Athens where Meg would continue to care for this man albeit married, who had found a way into the city of her heart. After the Germans had retreated and Stavros was discharged from the hospital, Athens was in turmoil so their illicit liaisons were conducted wherever and whenever there was an opportunity. She thought that they would have a future, that he would leave his wife and come back to England with her. Once, after another passionate encounter, he told her his wife was a vindictive and haranguing harpie. However, his Orthodox religion did not condone divorce and he could not bring himself to forsake his vows and abandon his wife. She would be waiting for him to return to their farm in Perivolaki to assist with the goat milking and cheese making which she had to manage herself while he was fighting in the war.

He had told her of his life there, the customs of the Greek people, their superstitions, women giving other women the evil eye, the sprinkling of holy water and basil to ward off the evil sprites who would surface from underground except for the twelve days of Christmas. The spring lamb eaten at Easter, the community ensuring the poverty stricken also had some to consume. On Sundays, everyone would dress in their best clothes and dance and sing. They would all join hands and dance around in a circle with a slow measured step at the same time singing in a shrill, nasal tone. When men were present, they began the song and the women would repeat it after them. Meg would visualise the scenes and wish she could be there with her Stavy joyously singing and dancing for gaiety was what was missing from her life. She could scarcely remember what it was like to dance and sing with utmost abandon. So far, her life had been steeped in blood, bombs, and tears. Even now there was little semblance of peace in Athens. Greece was in ruins along with the economy and groups of communists had started to form, the main one being the EAM, The National Liberation Front. There had been rumours that there would be violence so both she and her lover had determined to leave as soon as possible.

"Agapi mou, my darling," he whispered wrapping his arm around her as the sounds of marauding mobs drifted under their window.

"You know that I always love you."

"Oh, Stavy, I can't bear it," she sobbed. "I will never see you again. You are my soul mate, my everything. Please, please, come with me."

"No, agapi, it is useless, I cannot. I have made my decision, I must return to my wife, to farm."

He stroked her hair, black as a raven's wing through which he would run his fingers."You are only young," he told her, adding, "and, now the war is over, there will be someone else to love and have his children."

In her heart she knew what he was saying was true. There would not be a future for them. Her parents would never have countenanced such a union as they were as religious as Stavros, especially her mother, attending Mass every Sunday rosary in tow.

She turned then away from him but held his hand under the sheet. She could not bear to look upon his sweet face now bristled and in need of a shave. She thought about all the shaves and bed baths she had given him as he lay in his hospital bed. The tending of his wounds in the cave at Chania. They would all be memories to be cherished until she was unable to recall them.

She was awake when the first rays of light filtered through the curtain. Her thoughts turned to the night's passion in which they had indulged, their final conjoining of their bodies, feeding off each other as though providing themselves sustenance for the futures without each other. He, to return to the farm and his wife and she, to her childhood home in England. He had arranged with his friend to give him a lift in his car as far as Arakli and from there depending on how his leg felt he would either walk or wait for the bus.

He arose.

She watched him limp to the tiny bathroom.

She heard the tap running, the scrape of the razor on his face.

Why doesn't he say something?

He returned to the bedroom and commenced dressing.

"Why won't you talk to me?" Don't I mean anything to you now?" she cried sitting up in the crumpled sheets her face streaked with tears.

"It's better this way. I do not trust myself to talk as I might say things which will make it harder to leave."

She tried to understand. Maybe this way was the best for them. A fast parting, not a drawn out one.

He opened the door to the approaching day in Alexandras Avenue.

She padded over in her nightdress the one he had peeled from her and would never again.

"Take care and travel safely," he said kissing her on the cheek, an innocent kiss, a kiss you would place on a child or a relation not on a lover who had been stroked and touched in the most private of places.

Then he was gone, departed from her life for ever and she was left alone to shoulder her grief which she thought would be insurmountable.

She shut the door.

She needed some sort of sustenance but could not face food. Coffee was all she would be able to manage. As she desultorily poured the granules into the briki and added the water her thoughts flew to him. Was he safe travelling with his friend or would they be attacked on the way? Where would they stop for food and coffee? Was he missing her? She wondered if he was feeling as she was, unable to eat. She did not even have a photograph of him; she would have to make do with the memory of his hands, his dark eyebrows which she would stroke, his breath on her neck. All gestures to be taken with her on her solo journey homeward.

The coffee boiled, she added some sugar and sat forlornly at the little table over which they had held hands and spoke of their shared war experiences and other inconsequential things specific to them. He, however, always careful not to mention any future plans which would include her. The coffee seemed to have a somewhat calming effect even though she could hear distant shouting outside. She finished the coffee and threw herself into the business of tidying and cleaning up. She wandered into the bathroom and peered into the sink noticing the tiny bristles he had shaved from his face then, next to the sink lo and behold, his dog tag. He had forgotten to take it! She pounced on it and drew it to her lips to bring herself close to him, her darling. Oh, thank God, he had forgotten it, now I have a memento to always keep, to treasure. It would better than a photo, she thought, knowing his image would be permanently engraved in her mind. Taking the treasure, she went straight to her suitcase and placed it there where she would later secrete it among her underwear. Somewhat uplifted by the discovery, she tore the passion-stained sheets from the bed and stuffed them together with the towels into the basket to be taken to the laundry by a woman whom they had befriended, a refugee grateful to earn a few drachma to feed her children. She, like many others all living in this aged condominium in central Athens. The building with its thin walls through which could be heard the sounds of love and hate, the essence of humanity. The cracks through which emanated garlic vapours and roasted meat which now she found she could not tolerate. They had been fortunate to have sourced somewhere to stay away from the mayhem, immersing themselves in a cocoon of love. Stavros' comrade, Nico, the lessor, was recuperating in hospital with a severe wound to his back. Her thoughts segued to the time remaining, only a few hours until she would depart from Greece to her home, her parents, and her future as she had managed to obtain a passage on the Nea Hellas which had been turned into a troop ship. She could not envisage a future devoid of Stavros, this bringing a fresh round of tears. How was she to bear living again with her parents in that cluttered house in Putney filled with ephemera where there would be an enfilade of questions fired at her especially about her time in Chania? She intuited how they would be treating her as though she were still a child to be protected from the ravages of society. She, a grown woman who had endured and seen unspeakable things, had stood up to the Germans in her Red Cross uniform and survived the war. She envisaged her bedroom, the pink chenille bedspread, the picture of the Sacred Heart on the wall looking down at her, the sinner. She could imagine her parents' reaction if they had discovered that she was no longer a virgin, that she had lain with a man. The admonishments, the names she would be called, the pleading for her to hasten to church to seek forgiveness. Maybe there would be no house to go to. Hitler's bombs might have demolished it. It had been a while since she had heard from her parents, the postal service always delayed. She had sent them a telegram advising she was booked on the Nea Hellas but had received no reply. As much as she disliked her parents' constraints and attitude, she loved them and did not wish them any ill will and prayed that they would still be alive.

"Yassou," shouted a voice at the door interrupting her reverie.

It was the refugee come to collect the washing.

"Yassou, efharisto," replied Meg as she gave her the basket and the drachma lying in wait on the table.

They were the only words the two of them spoke, "hello and "thank you."

Meg felt embarrassed standing there in her nightdress with her hair awry and blotchy face but was unable and unwilling to try to explain to this woman what had transpired this morning. How her lover had fled to return to his wife leaving her to navigate an uncertain future in England.

However, the woman had more things to worry about than the unkempt vision before her and with an incline of the head, took the money stashing it in her apron pocket. She and the basket then made their way out into the street and away down the alley to the laundry.

Chapter Four

Larissa station was packed with people like her all clamouring to escape Athens. She had begun walking there with her suitcase but a couple had seen her distress and pulling their car over offered her a lift. She had been so grateful to them and collapsed on the back seat with her bag. In answer to their question, she had told them she was embarking on the Nea Hellas to return to London. In broken English they had told her they had relatives who owned a small restaurant in Camden and were also planning to leave Greece and live with them. They wanted to know more about her, what had she been doing in Greece during the war and what were her future plans. Her replies to these questions were very basic. She did not want to discuss too much of her experiences. She told them only she had been a nurse in Greece and was returning to her home in England.

At last, they arrived at the station. Thanking them profusely, she joined the throng boarding the train to the port. There were no vacant seats so she had to stand. As the train clanked down the line a feeling of light-headedness descended until all went black.

She came to on a seat which an English soldier had offered, her head between her knees.

"Oh, I am so embarrassed," she said to him after she had somewhat recovered.

"I should have eaten something this morning."

He took from his pocket some nuts which he handed to her.

"Eat some of these."

"Oh, thank you, you are so kind."

"You going to Piraeus?"

"Yes, are you?"

"Seems like the whole train is going," he replied.

She ate a few more nuts which made her feel slightly better as the train swayed and racketed along.

"I'm going on the Nea Hellas, to England," she said.

"So am I."

"I suppose there will be a lot of troops on board and the accommodation will be basic."

There was no reply to this. He was like her, non-committal, not saying too much which suited her as now she did not want to answer questions.

They soon arrived at the port and there was somewhat of a stampede to alight from the train.

Meg picked up the suitcase.

"I will carry it," he said. "You don't look like you're capable."

“Oh, alright, thank you. I must say, I don’t feel all that well.”

They commenced walking towards the wharf where lay the hulking form of the ship.

“There she blows,” announced the soldier.

“Oh, so it is,” replied Meg hoping she would soon feel better and be able to cope on the high seas all the way to England like she did when she volunteered. It is probably due to all the stress I have endured and the little food I have eaten she told herself unable or unwilling to think about whatever else it could be.

They joined the queue at the dock, Meg casting her eyes over the assembled multitude. There were the ubiquitous soldiers with their kit bags, mothers with crying babies in their arms, men both young and old whose faces held a mixture of apprehension and sadness. The latter had endured and survived this terrible war and now had to leave their homeland to forge a new future in another country. They moved closer to the official who perused the passengers’ paperwork Meg thinking that at least she was returning to a familiar place, to the country where she was born albeit to live with her parents.

“Papers, please.”

Meg proferred her passport and ticket.

The official studied them ensuring she was the one whose picture was on the passport.

Then it was the soldier's turn and, formalities completed, they clambered up the gangplank and onto the ship.

They parted ways but before he disappeared into the milieu of his ilk, he told her his name was Jimmy and maybe if it was alright, they could meet up for tea later in the dining room.

"Ok," she replied after giving her name to him thinking it would be harmless enough.

One of the crew directed her to the minute cabin which she was to share with a woman who was now sitting on the bottom bunk looking at a diary.

"Hello," said Meg putting down her suitcase relieved to be free of it.

"Looks like we will be cabinmates."

"Yes, hello," said the woman.

"I have taken the top bunk. I hope you don't mind."

"No, I would prefer the bottom," Meg intuiting it would be more convenient if she had to use the bathroom in the middle of the night or they had to abandon their cabin at short notice.

"I am Helen." The woman extended her hand which Meg shook noticing how soft it was so unlike her hands which were rather rough and chapped due to the extensive use of carbolic soap in the hospitals.

The ship began to creak. They heard and felt the engines rumble as the Nea Hellas left the dock.

"I think we are off," said Helen. "And God save us."

They both knew their voyage would be fraught with danger. They were in a convoy of seven ships as there were plenty of Japanese submarines lurking around ready to launch torpedoes.

“Don’t bother unpacking your night attire,” said Helen as Meg commenced to take her nightdress from the bag.

“Oh, why not?”

“We must sleep in our clothes in case of an attack during the night.”

Meg started to wonder then if she had made the right choice to leave Greece. It was either stay and be killed by the marauding communists or be torpedoed on this ship by the Japanese. However, she had survived the onslaught of the Germans so hopefully her luck would hold out a bit longer.

Meg returned her nightdress to the suitcase. Maybe it was better not to be wearing it as it would only conjure up memories of those passionate nights with her lover. She wondered if he had arrived safely. Did his wife welcome him into her arms as Meg would have done smothering him with kisses and sweeping him off to bed or was he rounding up the goats to be milked? Oh, how she missed him!

“What is the purpose of your voyage?” asked Helen as she cast her eyes on Meg’s left hand thinking she might sight a wedding ring.

“Oh, I’m returning home to England.”

“What part?”

“Putney, to my parents’ house actually.”

"It will be strange to live there again after my war experiences," she added.

"Oh, yes?" queried Helen.

"I was a nurse in Crete and Athens."

"My goodness," exclaimed Helen.

"You must have had a most awful time and seen some shocking things, but good on you my dear for doing what you did. I must say I could not have done it."

"Thank you," replied Meg.

"And, what about you?"

"I'm returning to my only son who has been pining away in boarding school for the duration of the war. My husband had to stay on in India as he is in the Medical Service."

"Oh, I see."

"Yes, and talking of India, do you know there are Italian prisoners on board who had been interned there?"

"Really? But now you mention it I thought I noticed when we were boarding, some foreign types in grey uniforms with a sort of black diamond on their backs."

"That would be them," said Helen.

Meg was feeling again lightheaded.

"Sorry, but do you mind if I go to the dining room? I haven't eaten properly today and I feel a bit subpar."

"We will both go," said Helen taking her handbag off the bunk.

"I am feeling a bit peckish myself."

Making their way out of the cabin, they walked along corridors until they found the dining area which was already filled with the clamour of humanity.

They found room at a table and perused the menu which to Meg's surprise was comprehensive.

"What do you feel like?" asked Helen.

"Oh, I don't know, it all looks delicious."

"I can recommend the ribs of beef with horseradish for a main and if you're hungry the chicken and ham patties are very good too."

Meg was unsure. Although she was hungry, she did not want to overindulge as she was unsure if her stomach could cope.

"I think I will have the cold celery essence and the fish."

"Ok, I will order the beef."

Helen signalled the waiter who took their order and hurried away to the kitchen.

Meg could feel the rocking of the ship and hoped that her stomach would not react. She told herself it was just the lack of food which was making her nauseous.

She took a drink from her water glass and surveyed the room wondering if that Jimmy fellow was present. To her surprise he was seated at a table in the corner talking to someone who looked like another army type. She quickly looked away but not before she noticed her giving a nod in her direction. She shyly smiled back and then the soup was brought to the table and her concentration was diverted.

Although it was cold, it tasted delicious and refreshing, a panacea to the heat which was all pervasive.

"Do you know," said Helen, cutting a piece of beef. "Not long after we left India, an oil tanker near us was torpedoed and caught on fire? There was smoke everywhere. At Aden, we picked up the survivors who were black with oil and wrapped in sheets. The crew came scrounging for some clothes for them to wear."

"Oh, how awful for them," said Meg glancing over to see if Jimmy was still looking at her but he was busy making inroads into his main meal his knife and fork both keeping time.

"Yes, it was, but thank heavens there wasn't any blood. I can't stand the sight of it I'm afraid. Not like you, a nurse. You must have had your fair share of that I imagine."

The mention of blood set Meg's mind awhirl. She had overlooked the fact that her monthlies had not arrived. However, with all the stress of the war they had been rather sporadic so it had not been a concern. But now it was. All her symptoms were pointing to the inevitable. Dear God, this was why she felt sick, she should have known, how stupid of her not to know, and she a nurse! She was carrying Stavros' child! What was she going to do? Her parents would totally disown her, cast her out to some unmarried mothers' place to give up her baby for adoption. Her and Stavros' baby. No, she could or would not do it. She had to come up with a plan and fast.

"What? Oh yes, we did but it was all par for the course," replied Meg hardly able to concentrate on what Helen was saying. All she could think of was a baby growing inside her.

"Do you still feel unwell?" asked Helen. "Only you have gone a little pale."

"Oh, have I?" Meg said touching her cheek "It must be some germ I picked up. The place where I was staying left a lot to be desired, I'm afraid."

"Well, if it would help, I have some seasickness tablets in the cabin."

"You are so kind, thanks very much. If I feel worse, I will take some."

"Goodoh," said Helen.

The waiter brought the main course.

Meg knew she must try to eat at least some of it. If nothing else, it would surely make her feel better.

As she took a bite of the flounder the cogs of her mind turned and then engaged with the plan which she knew was the only one which might save her from her dire predicament.

Chapter Five

"I wonder how long until she will be here?" asked Gwenyth, Meg's mother, placing three spoonfuls of tea into the pot.

Her husband Roger looked up from the racing section of the paper.

"I suppose we will just have to wait until she knocks on the door."

Gwenyth brought the pot over to the table and commenced pouring the tea.

"Yes, I suppose you are right. I hope and pray she will be safe. There are still lots of Japanese submarines lurking about. I wish she could have stayed in Greece a bit longer at least until things settled down a bit."

She brought the cup of tea over to her husband.

"Do you want a slice of that cake I made?"

"Wouldn't mind," Roger replied noisily slurping his tea.

"I do wish you wouldn't make that noise when you drink your tea Roger, it sounds terrible."

She took the cake from the tin and sliced two pieces, one for him and one for her then brought it over placing the plate on the small table next to him.

She sat down on the settee with her tea. Through the window were the ravaged remains of the other houses the occupants either dead or moved on to other accommodation. God had answered her prayers saving their house from Hitler's onslaught and she thanked Him every day, especially in Church where she attended every Sunday. She also thanked Him for sparing the Church which sustained only a minimum of damage to the roof. If they had been living in London, they might not have even survived so relentless had been the bombing. She remembered the day of her dental appointment near Russell Square having to pick her way over debris and broken glass past someone's bathroom whose toilet and sink were linked together making her want to cover it up to restore its dignity. Knives and forks glinted in the rubble among blue and white fragments of a serving dish. When Roger set off every day to his job at the insurance office she could not settle until his key was in the door and he was safely home.

The Church was the same one in which she married Roger which seemed like only yesterday. She in a cloche hat and a borrowed feather boa. He in a three -piece grey suit both being rained on by flurries of confetti. He had been one of the lucky ones who had returned from the War unscathed apart from some shrapnel lodged in his back which would be a permanent reminder of the War in years to come. However, she had thought it was a small price to pay, at least he had survived not like most of his and her friends whose shattered bodies lay scattered in the fields of France. His best friend Eddy was one of those souls. They were all part of a group from the same village in Sussex the group to which Gwenyth belonged. Roger had been her second choice; her true love had been Eddy. This had come to the fore on their wedding night she telling him of her fear of the marital act, of terrible things which might happen to her, the marriage remaining unconsummated until a few weeks after the honeymoon which had been in a guest house at Bournemouth by the sea. Her embarrassment was extreme when they repaired to the dining room everyone present knowing they were the "honeymooners" with their winks and snide remarks especially at breakfast. It had taken a toll on their relationship she even opining whether she should have married at all but it was the only way she would be able to have a child her maternal urge unable to be quelled. She wondered how on earth a baby could emerge from such a tiny opening and it took all her fortitude when Roger had been finally able to enter it. However there had been no pleasure for her. She had been sore and disappointed after he rolled off satiated and snoring beside her. But it had all been worth it when her darling daughter Meg was born. A premature birth, Gwenyth nearly delivering her in the shower which had been mandatory along with the enema and the shave. They had taken the baby away and wrapped her scrawny pink body in cotton wool atop her head, a woollen cap.

Months went by with no intimacy between husband and wife as all her concentration centred on the mewling infant who greedily sucked at her nipples every four hours.

"Why don't you put her on the bottle for heaven's sake?" said Roger when he awoke to find her crying in the night.

"You don't understand. I need to bond with her."

"But at what price? You are up and down all night and you're always complaining your breasts are sore."

"And talking of breasts. When are we going to resume our relations?" We haven't had any for months."

"You know it takes a while for everything to settle down Roger. How would you like to give birth feeling like a watermelon is coming out of you."

He stalked back to bed and left her with the baby.

Surely, he thought as he thumped the pillow to make it more comfortable, it can't be like this with every couple who has children. How much longer would he have to wait for some "how's your father"? She has not got any time for me. It is all about the baby. He would try and broach his concerns the next time he meets one of his friends at the pub. Dave should know something. Him with the three kids and another on the way. However, he could not divulge all details about his marriage, how long it took for the consummation. He would not want to feel as though it was his fault, not up to the job. He had thought that perhaps it had been him. Maybe he should have been more forthright, but he had been as inexperienced as her floundering around not knowing what was expected.

"It's my turn to do the Church today," Gwyneth announced getting up from the settee taking her cup, saucer and plate to the kitchen.

Roger mumbled something from behind his paper.

That was another irritation, all she seemed to think about was the Church. It was either attending choir practice two nights a week or dusting and polishing the brass and arranging the flowers on Saturday. Today was polishing day which he did not mind so much as it would give him a bit of time for himself, a chance to visit the SP bookie and place some bets on a few nags. This he would do surreptitiously as gambling was anathema to her. A thing to be frowned upon. He went to Church with her on Sundays under sufferance afterwards admonishing himself for not standing up to her refusing not to go. But he needed some peace in his life so went along genuflecting and kneeling, singing the hymns and receiving Communion. He had lost his faith on the blood- soaked battlefields. How could a God condone all the suffering he had witnessed? All the young bodies blown to pieces lying in the quagmire. What sort of a God was that? All the holy pictures festooning the house were also an affront to him. The crucifix hanging over their bed, the sacred heart on the wall in Meg's old bedroom. He wondered what her reaction would be when she returned. She a nurse, a witness to the atrocities of war. Would she like him also be a non-believer?

Another irritant was all the knick knacks which covered nearly every dresser and table. Silver spoons garnered from thrift shops, ashtrays and ornaments souvenired from various places all jostled for space among vases and bowls, the whole accumulating dust which was irregularly removed. He was at a loss to understand how she could devote so much time dusting and polishing the Church and hardly any to thoroughly cleaning their house.

"I'll leave you a cheese and pickle sandwich." she said now from the kitchen.

"Right," he replied circling Secret, a horse carrying ten to one odds in the third race. The name sounded ominous; it might even be a winner. He could not be classed as a winner as he thought about the secret he had kept from his wife, the illicit affair he had had during his marriage when he had felt abandoned and frustrated. She had been one of his co- workers at the insurance company where he was employed. With her come hither looks, tight skirts and jumpers which displayed her hour glass figure she had been just what he had been craving. He thought it would be just a one- night stand to prove to himself that he was still attractive to the opposite sex. However, she had mesmerised him, had listened to his concerns, had acquiesced to his fetish of having his toes sucked, and given blow jobs something his wife would never countenance. During the war, one of his comrades had been given a blow job by a French brothel worker leaving his penis covered in blisters so he had never partaken. He had heard that these women harboured diseases like syphilis and gonorrhea which in some cases led to loss of vision, brain damage and even death. But because his lover was an everyday housewife and not a prostitute, he thought that he was safe.

The indiscretion continued for six months then was abruptly terminated when his paramour's husband came home from rehabilitation finally recovered from a wound received in the war. He opined she had been probably as frustrated as he, so had justified his behaviour as a mutual service but in his heart, he had known it was wrong. He had forsaken his marital vows," for better or for worse." However, his urges were immutable leading to the services of a prostitute who satisfied his needs apart from the blow jobs from which he abstained his paranoia still residing in the foothills of his mind. His fetishes then evolved into dressing in women's underwear which the Madam accommodated as she wielded a cane onto his scantily clad backside. He had secreted a range of bras and panties in the back of his wardrobe to be donned whenever his wife was engaged with her Church activities.

Chapter Six

By the time the Nea Hellas entered the Suez Canal Meg and Jimmy were a couple. Like a spider enticing a fly into its web Meg had used every while at her disposal to kindle a romance between her and him. She had waited after dinner that first night until Helen had repaired to the cabin to make her move. She had sidled over and sat down next to him striking up a conversation immersing herself in his answers to her questions, feigning a coquettish look which was one of her talents. She was not proud of herself, felt a traitor to Stavros, her true love, as she let this other soldier have his way with her firstly in the lifeboat then in his cabin.

Helen seemed to know what was afoot as her cabin mate was spending less time with her and more with the soldier.

"I hope you know what you are doing," she said one day when Meg had returned to collect some fresh underwear.

"What do you mean?"

"Well, these shipboard romances. They are alright on the high seas but hardly ever lead to anything permanent."

“We’ll see,” said Meg turning over in her bunk hoping that her plan would come to fruition and solve the problem in her belly. She determined that the birth would be announced as premature to allay any suspicions which might surface.

She also hoped they would all survive this voyage as there had been submarines being chased by other boats in the convoy, the Nea Hellas shuddering as depth charges went off. Every day bombing raids occurred from the dreaded Swastikas as the Germans made their way to Italy. The many raging storms and gales turned the sea into a maelstrom sending most of the passengers to shelter in their cabins. She was thankful that her nausea had subsided unsure if it was due to the sea sickness tablets offered by Helen. There was boat drill every day and with life jackets donned it was another opportunity for Meg to position herself close to Jimmy. They were only allowed one bath a week but because the water was desalinated and smelt strange Meg did not miss more regular ablutions. The washbasins in the cabins sufficed for quick fresheners.

When they arrived at the Mediterranean end of the canal at Port Said thousands of American troops came out on landing crafts to board the ship. In their khaki helmets and bulging kit bags they climbed the rope ladders and swung themselves up and over the side of the ship.

“I hope there will be enough food for all of us,” said Meg as she observed with Jimmy the influx of Americans.

"I am all the food you will need," replied Jimmy giving her backside a pinch then her neck a nuzzle.

"Very funny, I'm sure," said Meg pushing a stray tendril behind her ear as a breeze wafted around the deck.

"And" he added, "if I catch you talking to any of those yanks there will be hell to pay. You know what they say about them don't you?"

"No, what do they say?"

"They are overpaid and oversexed."

Was he being serious or flippant warning her about the Americans? She was unsure but she would stay out of their way not wanting anything to jeopardise her relationship with him which was now becoming more serious. The last thing she wanted was to get involved with another man. A couple of nights ago after another passionate encounter in his bunk there were words spoken of love and even a future in England. It had been music to her ears, was what she had planned that fateful night when she had realised her condition.

Was it a proposal? It sounded like it was, but she needed to hear something official to set her mind at rest. She wondered if she would eventually come to love him as, at the moment, she only felt an affection, a means to an end not like the pure love she had with Stavros. However, she had heard that people in arranged marriages learnt to love one another, some after only meeting for a period of fifteen minutes. The same might happen for her. She wondered where they would be living. How far would they be from her parents' house? He intimated there would be a job awaiting at the bank in Fulham where he had worked before the war. Would that be where they would live, in a flat in Fulham?

It was when they had glimpsed the Rock of Gibraltar and joined an enormous convoy of ships, battle ships, destroyers and troop carriers who were en route bringing supplies for D Day that Meg told him she thought she might be pregnant. He seemed non plussed, had taken it in his stride believing it was his baby growing in her womb. Meg was anxious to legalise it as soon as possible to seek out the captain for an onboard marriage so she could face her parents as a married albeit pregnant woman.

To her relief, the captain and more importantly Jim agreed to her proposal and on one of the coldest grey days as the Nea Hellas steamed towards the coast of America, they were pronounced husband and wife.

"I wish the two of you a long and happy life," Helen said after the short ceremony at which she had been a witness intuiting that her cabinmate was probably in the family way due to the hasty wedding. Her eyes navigating towards Meg's stomach trying to detect some sign of a bump.

"Thank you," replied Meg hoping the wish would be fulfilled, that their relationship would evolve into something more than what she felt now. However, the only thing that mattered was the happiness and welfare of the child she was carrying. Stavros' child, the only memento she had of her true love. That would be her main focus and would remain so until the day she died.

"Will you have a proper wedding when you arrive home?" Helen enquired as the ship rolled and bucked sending their celebratory drinks sliding across the table.

Meg looked at Jim who did not offer an answer.

"Oh, I don't know," replied Meg. "We will probably just have a small get together in the pub. And with all the shortages of materials I can't imagine being able to get my hands on much of an ensemble."

"Yes, you are right to consider that," said Helen.

They discussed the route of the ship. Why they had steamed towards America when they were going to England Jimmy offering that it was to avoid the U boats which were ubiquitous.

Helen said, "I suppose now you are a married couple you will be sharing Jim's cabin until we dock."

"Yes, that's right," replied Jim pulling Meg closer to him much closer than she liked. It was as if he was ensuring she did not stray now she was married to him.

"It will be our honeymoon love nest won't it, sweets?"

It was the first time he had called her that and she was not sure she liked it. Stavros's name for her was Agapi Mou, my darling.

"Yes, Jimmy it will," she agreed.

As though in a haze, their married days passed in his cabin. They only ventured out to the dining room for meals, he accompanying her every time, always ensuring her eyes did not stray to any other men in the vicinity, especially the yanks. His appetite for sex had heightened since their betrothal but it was not like their initial love making or the love she had made with Stavros who had been always mindful of her feelings and pleasure. Now it was hard and fast leaving her in a morass of puzzlement, frustration and hurt. Was he trying to expunge the foetus in her womb?

Chapter Seven

"Welcome home!" announced Kevin holding aloft a festive balloon as Theo and Meg emerged with the other incoming passengers into the arrivals area at Heathrow.

"Good trip?"

"Oh, yes, Kevin it was unbelievable, especially Crete," enthused Meg her face alight with joy.

"Great. You will have to tell me all about it when you come over."

Theo pushed the trolley with their luggage as Kevin carried Meg's carry- on bag, Meg dawdling along behind them her progress slowed by her condition and the cramped conditions of the plane.

She felt somewhat bereft, disappointed that she was back in England after the time spent in the summer sun with Theo. She was back to the dismal leaden London days which she knew would only be made worse by her condition about which she had told Theo. She had been unable to hide it from him especially when he had sighted her swallowing the prescribed pain killers prior to their dinner in Chania.

"Why are you taking these mum?"

"Oh, I'm taking them for the pain I sometimes have. You know I am an old lady and subject to aches and pains."

"But mum, these look to be quite strong," said Theo after perusing the box and the prescribed label.

"Well, I only take them when I need to. Now come on. We don't want to miss our cocktails and the sunset."

Puzzled, Theo summoned a taxi which transported them back to the beautiful harbour at Chania. Meg took Theo's arm down the cobblestoned alleys they had traversed at lunchtime then on towards the Fortress and the Pallas restaurant which was already crowded with people.

After Theo advised the maitre d of their reservation, they were shown to their table which to their joy had an uninterrupted view of the lighthouse.

"I will order a Margarita," said Meg settling into her chair as a waiter glided over.

"Do you think that's wise if you are taking those tablets. It said on the box not to drink alcohol when you are taking them."

"Fiddlesticks. I intend to enjoy myself tonight so to hell with all that nonsense."

"Ok then mum, on your head be it."

"A Margarita for my mother and an Aperol for me, thank you."

The waiter minced off with their order.

Meg patted her son's hand.

"Thank you, Theo for a wonderful holiday. I will never forget it."

"It was good, wasn't it?" We didn't miss a beat."

"And that hotel in Paris! I felt like a celebrity and no mistake."

"Well, you deserved it mum, after everything you have been through"

Their drinks were brought.

"Cheers, to us," said Theo as they clinked glasses.

Menus were flourished.

"Oh, no Theo. I forgot my glasses" said Meg after fossicking through her handbag to no avail.

"Don't worry. I will let you know what's on offer. What do you feel like?"

"I wouldn't mind a steak."

"Ok. Let's see. They have an Argentine rib eye served with parsnip puree and a mushroom sauce or a sirloin with pepper sauce and French fries."

"I will have the rib eye. It sounds delicious."

"What do they have as entrees?" she added.

"There's burrata or kingfish carpaccio."

"Ok."

"How about you have the burrata and I will have the carpaccio and we can share," suggested Meg hoping she would be able to eat everything.

"Good idea," replied Theo, "and I will order the rib eye and ask if I can have the pepper sauce instead of the mushroom."

The waiter returned and took their order adding a bottle of Balliamo Prosecco, a brand which Meg favoured.

They sipped their drinks. Meg licked the salt from the rim of her glass and looked across at the lighthouse as the orange orb began its descent below the horizon while the strains of Verdi wafted in the air.

"Oh, Theo," Meg exclaimed. "Isn't it magical?" Theo nodded almost as awestruck as his mother who he had noticed was wiping a tear from her eye so immersed was she in the wondrous scene. How glad he was that he was able to bring her here to Crete where she had spent time in the war. He wanted to find out more about that time. Was it here where she nursed the soldiers? Was that her main reason for wanting to come? Or was it just because it was a beautiful place? And what of that medication she was taking? It would not have been prescribed unless it was for something serious. He determined to extract more information from her at an opportune moment.

While her son was immersed in his thoughts Meg also was thinking, how she would savour every moment of this night, every morsel she ate, all the sips she would drink, every word she would share with her son. She would tell him a little about her experiences here in the caves of Chania albeit omitting anything about her relationship with her beloved Stavros. Should she tell him now at the end of her life when her days were numbered? Did he deserve to know who his real father was? She did not know what to do. She did not want to ruin her relationship with her son who had been so good to her especially organising this beautiful holiday. He might become angry with her and resentful that she had not told him earlier. Letting him think all these years that Jim was his dad.

After the sun had given up its glow and the steaks were eaten, Theo embarked on his quest to elicit information from his mother.

He took a good swig of wine then plunged in.

"Mum, please tell me the real reason why you are taking such strong medication."

Meg fingered the stem of her glass and looked towards the lighthouse silhouetted now against the violet hue of the sky.

She turned her gaze towards her son.

"Don't let's spoil our night Theo. I promise I will tell you in good time."

"Alright, but please make sure you do. I have a right to know, whatever it is."

The tiramisu arrived distracting them from any more consternation.

They both drove their forks into the creamy dish as they were sharing it.

In an attempt to divert Theo from his concern about her health Meg said,

"Would you like to know about what I did in the war?"

"Oh, yes, I certainly would, and it's about time you told me."

"Was it around here that you nursed?"

As she was stabbed by another pain which she hoped Theo had not noticed she told him about her experiences, of the perilous journey on the boat with the wounded soldiers, being wrecked on the island and rescued, of setting up the tent hospital and ultimately relocating to the caves not far from where they were now ensconced. She told him about the regular bombings in the harbour, the bodies of the soldiers who had died in the caves being dumped into the ocean, the day when they all thought they would be killed by the Germans who had discovered them in the cave. Their reprieve and the transportation to the hospital in Athens.

Theo was at a loss for words. He was in disbelief that his mother had endured such experiences and had survived to tell the tale. His admiration for her was boundless.

"Oh, mum," he said taking her hand which bore all the hallmarks of her age. The papery skin mottled with brown, like tiny pebbles in the snow.

"You deserve a medal!"

Meg smirked.

"I don't know about that Theo. I was just doing my duty just like everyone else who was there."

"God, it must have been terrible when those Germans arrived. You must have thought the game was up."

"Yes, I did and I thought I would rather have been machine gunned there and then rather than be put into one of their prison camps."

"Well, thank God you survived and went on to have me. I am so full of admiration for you mum and I must say I could not have done what you did. You are a hero."

Oh, Theo, she thought, if you only knew. I am far from a hero. I am a deceitful liar and not worthy of your admiration.

Their dinner now at an end, the bill was paid.

Theo assisted his mother up from her chair and, in the twilight, they wended their way from the idyllic scene back to the hotel.

It was after breakfast the next morning that she had told him of the cancer. She wanted him to have a good night's sleep after their beautiful dinner. Not to lie awake worrying about her condition.

"Oh, mum, I wish you had told me sooner."

"What would have been the use? At least we both had a wonderful holiday and I got to return to Chania. If I had have told you earlier you probably would have cancelled it all and bunged me into a hospital and we would have not had our amazing dinner."

"Yes, I suppose you're right," he said already consumed by the visions of the inevitable suffering she would endure leading to her eventual demise.

"How long did they say you have?" he ventured.

"Oh, a few months, give or take."

"Oh."

"Now don't get all gloomy and maudlin on me Theo. I have had a good innings until now so we must be grateful for that."

"Yes, mum, I know you have but I still don't want you to suffer."

"I will contact a hospice when we get back. I want you to have the best of care."

"No, Theo. I don't want to go to such a place. I want to stay in my own home."

Theo fingered his eyebrow, a mannerism specific to his reaction to stress.

"Are you sure about that mum?"

"Yes, Theo I am. I don't want to be in a hospice and that's the end of it."

"Well, alright if that's what you want but I will engage a nurse to come in and look after you."

A compromise had been reached which had put her mind at rest. She had even given Theo a handwritten list about what she requested for her funeral. Naturally, Theo would be the celebrant, the hymns, Morning Has Broken, How Great Thou Art, the floral arrangement atop the casket to be a mixture of white roses and baby's breath interspersed with green myrtle or ivy. Suitable for cremation, her casket was to be a pale oak wood veneer with her ashes scattered in the sea at Chania. Now unencumbered without the vexing problems which had being plaguing her, she reclined on the settee, with her thoughts, her diary, the painkillers and Tiddles snuggled beside her.

Chapter Eight

It was on a grey chill March morning that the Nea Hellas weighed anchor in the Firth of Clyde in Scotland after being rerouted from the American coast. The passengers were ordered to take their cabin baggage and assemble on deck at the lifeboat stations. Then the order was given to climb down over the ship on rope ladders to the landing craft below.

"God, I hope I don't fall," thought Meg as she hoisted herself onto the first rung of the ladder Jim already halfway down.

"I wish he had waited for me," she added as her feet gingerly made contact with the proceeding rungs. As she descended, she caught sight of the quarantine flag streaming in the breeze knowing it was alerting the authorities that the ship's cook had caught polio. This had made her anxious to be off the ship and away from any disease or contamination which might affect her pregnancy. Finally, she was down and clambering into one of the boats in which her husband was sitting.

"You made it then?" he said moving up to make room for her.

"Yes, thanks but I thought you would have waited for me."

"I think it's every man for himself sweets, especially now there is polio on board."

She wished he would not keep calling her "sweets" but did not want to have any confrontation with him. She would just have to put up with it and bite her tongue as this is what she seemed to be doing now on a regular basis. Hadn't he heard about "women and children first?"

The waves tossed them about as the passengers attempted to pull more tightly around them the coats and wraps in an endeavour to obtain some warmth. Meg scanned the boat to see if Helen was aboard but she was not to be seen. She would have liked her company, to have another woman to talk to, to confide in, to ask her advice about her situation. However, Helen's words of wisdom had already been uttered when she expounded about "shipboard romances" not having any permanence. But Meg's situation was different. It was not a shipboard romance. She had tantalised and coerced Jim into marriage, so it was her problem to deal with. She felt shame at what she had done, her sleepless nights attesting to her turmoil but what choice did she have in her condition? Maybe his attitude towards me will improve when we are back in England in familiar surroundings, she thought as they were disgorged from the boat. In the chill and damp of a Scottish morning they made their way to the train station and at a greasy table in the small cafe conversation was providentially replaced by the consumption of fried eggs and ersatz coffee.

Soon they were alerted to the sound of the train lumbering in the distance and made ready to leave the confines of the café. Within the scrum of people on the platform Meg espied Helen. She waved to her, and Helen came over.

"Hello," she said.

"Hello Helen, I'm so glad I caught up with you. I was looking for you when we left the ship."

"I was one of the first to get off when I heard that the cook had contracted polio."

"Yes, wasn't that terrible? The poor man, I feel so sorry for him. I hope he will be alright."

"Me too. Wasn't it scary climbing down those rope ladders?" commented Helen. "I was sure I would land in the drink."

"Yes, I was scared stiff too, but we made it and here we are, safe and sound thank heavens."

Jim stood by his concentration on a cigarette precluding his need to add to the conversation.

They were assailed by the belching and smoking of the train as it drew up to the platform.

"Well, we better make a move and try to get a seat. By the look of all these people the train will be crowded," said Meg.

Jim took her bag and went on ahead leaving the two women trailing in his wake which offered Meg the opportunity to disclose to Helen the news of her pregnancy.

"Oh, really," she said. "That's wonderful news, congratulations. I hope everything goes well for you." She had been rather taken aback by the news and suspicious of the timing of it but who was she to point the finger? She had been pregnant before she had married her husband passing off the birth as premature.

"Thanks, so do I. But I am a bit worried about my parents' reaction. They don't even know I am married."

"Oh, I'm sure they will be fine knowing they will have a grandchild to spoil."

"Oh, I do hope you are right," replied Meg hopeful that would be the case, a grandchild to love and cherish.

"Would it be ok if I write to you sometime?" asked Meg.

"Yes, that would be lovely."

She withdrew a notebook from her bag and scribbled an address then gave it to Meg.

"Oh, thanks Helen, that's great. I will let you know my address when I write. Jim said we will be living in Fulham, but I don't know more than that I'm afraid."

They hauled themselves onto the train and Meg looked around the carriage for Jim who she noticed had secured what looked like the last vacant seat.

Helen, seeing how crowded the carriage was elected to go into the next one.

"If we miss each other I want to wish you all the best," she said planting a kiss on Meg's cheek.

"Thanks for everything Helen. It was lovely meeting you and I hope you have a great reunion with your son."

"Byee, and don't forget to write," said Helen pushing her way onward into the next carriage.

Meg approached Jim who moved over making room for her to sit down.

A whistle sounded, the train lurched and groaned, and they were finally on their way to married life in the suburbs of London.

Jim had told her they would be moving in with his parents in Fulham which did not instil any confidence in her. She wondered if his parents would be better than hers. Would their house be decorated in religious icons and ephemera? What would his mother be like? Would she dislike her presence in the house especially in the kitchen? How long would they have to stay with them? Even if they had to live in a room in a boarding house, she thought it would be preferable than living with a cantankerous mother-in-law. And what of his father who Jim had not mentioned. Would he be some ogre? Her imagination ran amok as the train chuffed along through the mist and the lochs of Scotland.

"Why don't you ever mention your father, Jim?" she asked.

He turned his head towards her.

"Don't need to talk about him," he replied.

“And if you know what’s good for you, just keep out of his way.”

“Why?”

“Just do as I say Meg.”

“Alright.”

That was the end of her questions. He had shut down the conversation leaving her more anxious and concerned. What was it about his father that Jim was unable to enunciate?

They sped by the stations leaving Scotland behind wreathed in mist and it was not long until they reached the outskirts of London, the grey drabness accentuated by the aftermath of the war.

“Not long now,” announced Jim after an interminable silence.

“No,” replied Meg as her feelings of anxiety of meeting his parents rose to greater heights.

What would be their reaction? Would they like or despise her? Would they see through her deception, her cuckolding of their son?

She had wanted to call at her house first to alert her parents of her matrimonial state, but Jim had not agreed maintaining that as he was her husband it was his prerogative that she accede to his demands. The visit to her parents would have to wait until the next day after they unpacked and settled into Fulham. She thought that as her parents were unaware of the time of her arrival in England, another day would not make much difference.

The train belched into Fulham. They gathered their belongings and exited the station.

"We can walk from here, it's not far," announced Jim taking her suitcase and striding ahead. With a somewhat heavy heart, Meg trailed along behind him her mind consumed with anxiety about meeting his parents and having to cohabit with them, the dour day and damaged buildings exacerbating her feelings of impending doom.

They were still on the high street with its motley collection of shops until she noticed Jim stopping at a fish and chip shop. Were they going to eat there she wondered?

"Come on, we're here," cried Jim as he waited for her to catch up.

"Are we having lunch here then?" she asked.

"No, sweets. This is where our digs are. Right on the top of the shop."

She was in disbelief. Surely, they would not be living on the top of this shop? Why didn't he tell her before?

He withdrew a key from his pocket and unlocked a dirty brown door alongside the entrance to the shop. They ascended the worn stairs Meg's stomach barely able to withstand the aroma of cooked fat permeating the air.

"Hoy there, ma," yelled Jim as a plump lugubrious woman materialised from the gloom. She looked like she was in a state of siege behind the intimidating ramparts of her breasts.

"Is that you, our Jimmy?"

"Yes, it's me safe and sound."

"And who's this?" she asked scrutinising Meg with her eyes like two raisins in a pudding.

"She's the wife. Meg is her name and we got hitched on the way over."

"How do you do?" said Meg extending her hand.

"Well, I'm not sure how I do and that's a fact."

"Now Ma, let's all get inside, and we can have a chin wag."

Meg followed Jim and his mother inside and was so grateful to sit down on the brown sofa she hardly noticed the springs poking into her backside.

"Well, if this isn't a turn up for the books Jimmy. You arriving here with a missus in tow."

She lit a cigarette and offered one to Meg who declined, her gaze drifting to the ashtray overflowing with butts.

"I'm Maud by the way," she said as the smoke added to the room's fug unable to escape through the unopened window shrouded by thick curtains. However, there was enough light for Meg to detect stains of nicotine on the ceiling which was peeling in various places.

"Suppose you're in the family way?"

Meg, cringing with embarrassment looked at her husband hoping he would answer that question, shame precluding her response.

"Had to make an honest woman of her, didn't I?"

"Thought as much. You were always the one who couldn't keep it in your trousers just like your old man."

"Where's he at the moment?"

“Where he always is. Down the pub getting sauced.”

Meg was dying for something to drink but did not want to ask for anything and was so relieved when his mother stubbed out the cigarette and put on the kettle for tea.

“How long you planning to stay?” she asked from the kitchen which Meg noticed was poky and would be unable to accommodate more than one person at a time.

“Don’t know. I have to get my old job back first, then we’ll see.”

“Well, there’s not much room here you know. You’ll have to sleep in the spare room which needs a good clean out. Your father has filled it up with gawd only knows what.”

Meg wondered what the room contained and if she would be expected to help haul out whatever it was.

A tray with cups and a pot of tea was brought into the room and placed on the small table which like the settee had seen better days evidenced by the stains and scratches on the surface.

“There’s nothing to eat with the tea. We ate the last of the biscuits and I wasn’t expecting visitors.”

“Well, get on then. Start pouring, Jimmy. I’m not the maid you know.” She admonished sitting back, resuming her smoking.

It was obvious that he and his mother were not close as up to now she had not enquired about his time in the war.

He handed Meg a cup. It was too hot to drink. She would have preferred some cool water but was too reticent to ask.

She blew on the tea to cool it down noticing the worn carpet displaying indeterminate stains. God, how was she going to stand living here? Her parents' house with her mother's ephemera and religious icons would be far more preferable than this hovel. She would even put up with the admonishments about her marital and pregnant state.

"Suppose you'll be wanting lunch?" Maud enquired.

"What's on offer?" he asked.

"Not much. As I say, I wasn't expecting visitors. There might be a bit of spam you could make a sandwich with."

"Your wife here can sort it out. Better start as you mean to finish, eh?"

What was that supposed to mean, thought Meg, having to make the lunch and Lord only knew what else?

She arose from the sofa her backside sore from the springs and made her way to the poky kitchen.

There was a bread bin on the counter. Meg peered into it and withdrew a half loaf which, to her eye, did not seem very fresh.

"There's some butter in the safe and spam's in the cupboard," Maud yelled from the gloom.

"Ok, thanks," she replied now searching in a drawer for the breadknife which was finally unearthed from an assortment of knives, forks and spoons jostling for space with boxes of matches, bottle tops and wads of greaseproof paper.

Meg set about cutting the bread on the counter as there was no evidence of a board on which to cut. She spread some butter then sliced the spam all the while knowing that her appetite was slowly diminishing. How on earth would she be able to swallow any of this?

As she brought the sandwiches into the room a key was heard turning the lock and in lumbered a corpulent, unshaven, and unkempt man replete with the florid complexion of a heavy drinker.

"So, you had enough down there then?" asked Maud.

"And here is our Jim," she added, "home from the war, and with a missus to boot."

Jim looked at his father and offered his hand, but no reciprocation was forthcoming. Instead, his father collapsed into the armchair wiping his mouth from which exuded a strong stench of beer.

"How many you kill over there?" he suddenly slurred turning his head towards his son.

"Didn't take you long to get hitched," he added, now directing his glance towards Meg who was now desperate to leave.

"Yes," piped up Maud. "And she's in the family way so you and me will be grandparents."

"Where you gonna live?" asked Alfie. "Hope you don't think you're staying here with some screaming brat."

A loud fart then emanated from him which echoed around the room.

"Ah, better out than in," said he.

Maud took a bite of a sandwich and said with her mouth full.

“He reckons we can put them up here until he gets his old job back.”

“Well,” slurred Alfie. “You better get cracking then sonny. There’s going to be lots more like you wanting jobs.”

Suddenly there was a loud knocking on the door.

“Cripes, who the hell is that? More visitors?” spluttered Maud stuffing the rest of the sandwich into her mouth and shuffling to the door.

“Is this the address of a Mr Alfred Lynch?” asked one of the two policemen, notebook in hand.

“Yes, and what’s he done now?” asked Maud.

Chapter Nine

"Do you fancy going to that new bar on Friday?" asked Theo who was in the kitchen pouring dressing over the salad.

"The one in Oxford Circus?" Kevin called out from the balcony.

"No, that one we passed by last week in Drury Lane."

"Oh, that one? Yes, I remember. But I think we should leave it for another night. Those places don't get going until about 11.00 and I will probably be ready for bed long before that."

"You're working too hard," said Theo.

"Can't be helped. You know I must get those billable hours if I want that promotion."

Theo wished Kevin would lower his enthusiasm for ascending the corporate ladder. Why could he not be content with the role he was now in? He was working too hard as it was and if he was a partner there would be more responsibility placed on him. He thought it was affecting his health as he seemed to be always contracting colds and flu to say nothing of his low libido. They had not made love for weeks. He was always too tired. Theo missed their intimacy, the times when they could not keep their hands off each other, leaping into bed whenever they had the chance. Now they were like an old married heterosexual couple and Theo hoped his lover was not becoming bored with him or worse, would take up with a woman as he had previously been married for ten years until he decided he was gay. That news had not gone down well with his parents leaving him alienated from them especially his father who had told him never to contact him again. His mother however always sent him a musical Christmas card as if she wanted to say more but did not know how. Theo could not bear if they broke up, having to return to the dating scene, the trawling around bars, the parties where he would inevitably drink too much and regret it the day after.

A bar was where they had met, some smoky basement jazz place frequented by types such as themselves, gay and on the lookout for a hook up. Kevin had approached him first Theo's reticence precluding him from making the first move.

"Got a light?" He had said waving a cigarette around in front of Theo.

"No, sorry, don't smoke."

"That's ok, think I've smoked enough already."

"What you drinking?"

"Whisky sour."

And with that Kevin had ordered two more, a straight whisky for him and another sour for Theo.

"Was that your usual pickup line?" Theo had asked him after they had downed the drinks and boarded the raft of conversation.

"What, asking for a light you mean?"

"Yes."

"As a matter of fact, I haven't used it in a while. Although, it still seems to do the job, as I managed to get your attention."

"Yes, I'd say you did."

They both chortled at that. It was one of the things they shared, a sense of humour, able to see the funny side of life. Initially, Theo was not keen to start another serious relationship as the previous one had ended badly, his lover accusing him of cheating and displaying signs of coercive control triggering memories of his father's abusive behaviour towards his mother. She always had reservations about this fellow, saying she thought he seemed shifty and untrustworthy, his dreadlocks adding to her distaste. He had been grateful for her perspicacity, her encouragement to break up with him. He also was grateful for her acceptance of his homosexuality, permitting him to bring his boyfriends to stay overnight in his room. He had been worried about telling her of his sexual proclivity, if she would cast him adrift and cut all communication with him. He had heard how this was the behaviour of some parents, and he could not have borne his mother severing all ties with him. However, he should not have been concerned as, after imparting the news, Meg had thrown her arms around him and said she had intuited a long time ago that he was gay and had been waiting for him to confirm her assumption. She had told him he had always been a sensitive child and shown no interest in playing with boys' toys preferring instead to rummage through Meg's jewellery box or pick wildflowers especially for her.

"I just want you to be happy with whomever you choose to be with," she had said. It had been such a relief for him to receive her blessing, a heavy weight lifted from his mind. He knew his father would have been abhorred by his gayness and would have probably given him a black eye or worse before throwing him out of the house and thoroughly disowning him. When Theo was a child, he had heard his father calling someone a "poofter" and he wondered what it meant.

Theo brought the salad out to the balcony where Kevin was sitting enjoying a glass of cab sav, watching the day end, the sky awash with blood red smears slowly widening to a flood as the strains of Ella Fitzgerald drifted from the sitting room.

"Thanks for preparing the supper," said Kevin taking hold of Theo's hand.

"No problem."

He sat down opposite Kevin and poured himself some wine.

"Cheers, then," said Theo rather dispiritedly.

Kevin noticed Theo's mood.

"What's wrong hon?"

Theo rubbed his eyebrow and fingered the stem of his glass.

"I'm concerned about you, about us."

"Concerned? Why?"

"You're working too hard for one thing, and I think it's affecting your health and, when was the last time we had sex?"

Kevin looked down at his plate and speared a buttered stalk of asparagus.

"You know I have to keep my shoulder to the wheel if I want to be a partner."

"But do you have to be? They will expect you to work even harder. There's more to life than making money."

"Yes, but if I don't make the big bucks we can't afford to live in this pad and enjoy our good wine and food such as this salmon which, I might add, tastes superb."

"Well, it should be. I bought it in Harrods."

"Exactly my point. You get what you pay for."

Kevin poured more wine into their glasses as Theo helped himself to the salad.

Casting about for another subject he asked about Theo's mother.

Theo took a big swig of wine thinking it was just like Kevin to segue onto something else and not address the problem which was upsetting their relationship.

"About the same," replied Theo. "She's on stronger medication now, the nurse told me."

"She hasn't changed her mind about going into the Hospice?"

"No, she's still adamant about staying put, amongst her things, where everything is familiar to her."

"Fair enough. At least she has a competent nurse. She probably would not receive any better care in a facility."

Theo hoped that was the case. The nurse certainly took great care of his mother ensuring that she was comfortable and increasing the pain medication as needed. He had asked her if she knew how long his mother would live but she had only an estimation of maybe a month or so. She had told him his mother's heart was strong and her will to live even stronger. Yesterday when he had visited, she had lapsed into a state of delirium, he hearing her say, "don't leave, my darling, no, no, the bombs." He had sat by her, held her hand and wiped her fevered brow with the damp cloth which the nurse left on the table. The war was still uppermost in her mind and would probably be there until the minute she died. Oh, how pleased he was that they were able to go on their final holiday together especially to beautiful Chania which his mother held so dear.

"You haven't told me about the highlight of your trip," said Kevin topping up their glasses.

"Oh, there were many memorable moments for mum especially our night in that beautiful hotel in Paris. She was beside herself and thought she was some class of celebrity!

But we both were entranced by Chania. I wish you could have experienced the wonder of the place; the Venetian lighthouse being pummelled by the waves as the sun set behind it. I swear darl, it was like a painting by Blechen."

Kevin sipped his wine and said,

"It was probably bittersweet for her knowing that she spent time there during the war. Did she say much about that?"

"Yes, after all this time, she spilt the beans. Apparently, she and the medicos had an awful time of it. They fetched up on a deserted island and then were rescued by another boat. She told me about the caves where they set up some sort of camp hospital to keep them and their patients safe."

"Jesus!" announced Kevin. "Your mum sure is a plucky one."

"Yes, she was but, here is the clincher. The Germans discovered them hiding out in the cave. She stood up to one of them pointing out her Red Cross uniform which probably saved her life."

"Well, good job they were the merciful sort and not like the Nazis otherwise she and the others would have been shot to pieces."

"Amen to that," said Theo. "And here's cheers to her and all the other heroes of the war."

They clinked glasses.

"I'm so glad you had a good holiday with your mum hon," said Kevin reaching over and stroking Theo's hand.

"I missed you when you were away."

"Well, I missed you too."

"Don't worry about us. When this case is completed, I promise we will have more time together. We might even have a dirty weekend at that hotel in Sussex."

"What, the one where I was celebrant at that wedding and walked in on the bridesmaid screwing the groom?"

"Yes, that one."

Theo had many interesting experiences as a celebrant and was in disbelief how some of humanity behaved. There were drunken brawls at weddings with chairs and punches thrown, grooms left waiting at the altar only to discover their betrothed had changed her mind. A funeral of a woman attended only by her two daughters one of them announcing her mother was a "fucking bitch' and they were only there to ensure she was truly dead and buried. He thought he could write a book about the things he witnessed and would call it, A Day in the Life of a Celebrant. Of course, there were many other happy and emotional occasions, one wedding in particular edged in his mind. It was conducted in a flower bedecked room in a hospital where a groom lay dying of muscular dystrophy his voice impaired, his breathing laboured. Dressed in a bridal gown and veil, the bride was beside him holding his hand. There was nary a dry eye in the room as their friends saw and heard recited the marital vows. He had been the celebrant at the groom's funeral. It had taken all his fortitude to stand there in the chapel in front of the attendees averting his gaze from the tear-stained face of the bride inconsolable at the loss of her husband having married him only five days before. Another occasion was the wedding of a bride who had been knocked off her bike by a car running a red light. A paraplegic in a wheelchair, she had been pushed down the red carpet by her proud father towards the groom who awaited with face beaming and eyes welling with unshed tears. The funerals of children he found the worst, especially babies, their tiny white coffins accompanied by stuffed toys and things which might entertain them, bring them joy in the next life. The white doves released into the sky as the coffins were lowered into the ground. He thought how he would cope with his mother's funeral, the scattering of her ashes at Chania. It would be hard but he would do it as she requested, to grant her this wish, to be with her in those her final moments. Thinking of that, he asked Theo.

"Mum wants me to be the celebrant at her funeral. She's given me a list of what she requires, hymns, flowers and so on and she also wants her ashes scattered in Chania.

"Oh, ok, how would you feel about returning there?"

Theo stroked his eyebrow and finished his wine.

"I don't think I could do it on my own, Kev. It would be too much."

Kevin rose from his chair and came around to Theo. Putting his arm around him he said,

You won't have to my love. I will pull out all stops and come with you."

"Oh, really?" Theo said standing up and giving him a hug. "That would make things a lot easier. Thank you."

"That's what friends do, isn't it?"

"Friends?" said Theo. "I hope we are a lot more than that?"

"I was only joking darl. You should know that. Now, enough of this, let us have that tiramisu I spied in the fridge and adjourn to the sitting room with a brandy."

"Sounds good," replied Theo his thoughts of a weekend away and Kevin's consenting to go with him to Chania restoring his mood to equanimity.

As they settled on the settee, Meg's nightmares continued to haunt her. Apocalyptic scenes of war, fire and devastation competed with visions of the camp hospital being obliterated by a bomb. It was when she saw pieces of her beloved Stavros scattered amongst the ruins that her screams summoned the nurse who hastened to the bedside to give her solace.

Chapter Ten

On the day after their homecoming, at the insistence of Meg, she and Jim had taken the train to see her parents. Her mother's shock at her hasty marriage and pregnancy had been palpable as Meg had known it would. Her father, however had been more accommodating, shaking Jim's hand and pouring out fingers of whisky to celebrate the news.

"But are you going to have a proper wedding?" Gwyenth asked, her hands tightly wrapped around the glass to still her nerves which were threatening to undo her. It had been her dream that her only daughter would walk down the aisle in virginal white in the church which she had festooned with the floral arrangements, the brass, and the pews she had polished. But it would not happen now. It would be drinks at the pub like some sort of wake which is what she was feeling. It was like a death, the death of her dream for Meg. She had scrutinised this new husband of hers trying to decide if he came up to standard. Apart from being a soldier and working at a bank what other attributes did he have? She noticed that for a newly married couple there did not seem to be a lot of loving interaction, the holding of hands, the gazing into each other's eyes, the completion of sentences. She also noticed a frisson of tension in her daughter. Was it because of her pregnant state, the concern that she would be disapproving of Jim?

He was not very communicative, and Gwyneth could not understand why Meg had been attracted to him in the first place. Her daughter had always attracted admirers and, when she volunteered to join the war effort as a nurse, Gwyneth hoped she would end up with a doctor but here she was married and pregnant to this banking fellow living above a shop, God help us! Her vivacity seemed to have disappeared replaced by a sort of meekness. Maybe it was all because of the war which she knew wreaked havoc with people's characters. She hoped that was the case and in the fullness of time her daughter's personality would be restored.

After another lull in conversation Roger asked them about their experiences in the war. Meg knew Jim would not want to talk about it so it was up to her to let them know. She concentrated on her training in London, the terrible voyage on the boat being strafed by guns, the stranding on the island and being rescued, the bombing by the Germans. When it came to the Chania caves and their love nest in Athens, it took all her strength to block out the image of her beloved, her Stavros the father of this child she was carrying.

They departed soon after with plans and promises to convene at the White Horse pub to celebrate their belated betrothal.

"I can't get over it," announced Gwyneth shutting the door on their retreating backs. She reached for the bottle of whisky and poured a good measure into the glass then downed it just as swiftly.

"How she got mixed up with the likes of him," she added.

"What's wrong with him?" Responded Roger.

"Just because he's not a doctor which was what you expected her to marry doesn't mean he won't be a good husband and father."

"There's something about him though," she said now reaching for the packet of cigarettes.

"Like what?"

"Well, for one thing, he doesn't look you in the eye when he talks and the two of them don't seem very loving."

"Bollocks. You can't expect them to be all over each other in front of us, can you and, as for looking you in the eye, I don't think that's much to worry about. Just be thankful she made it through the war which by what she told us was nothing less than miraculous."

She inhaled deeply on the cigarette and tried to take on board what her husband was saying but she could not shake the feeling she had about her daughter's husband. Maybe it was female intuition, but she was usually right about these things and this time she hoped and prayed that she would be wrong.

Chapter Eleven

A few weeks later, Meg decided to write a letter to Helen. She felt it would be cathartic, a chance to offload her anxieties to somehow cope with the situation into which she had fallen. She was being treated as no more than an unpaid servant, expected to cook and clean during the daylight hours then available as a sexual plaything at night for her husband. It did not matter that she was pregnant and tired from her duties. All that mattered was Jim's sexual needs were fulfilled. She thought he took after his father in that department as, through the thin wall, she would hear his nightly groaning and grinding as well as burping, farting and snoring.

She picked a time to write when the occupants were away. Maud to her bingo, Alf to someplace indeterminate and Jim to the bank (his old job reinstated).

2/34 High Street

Fulham

Dear Helen

I hope you have settled back into normal family life, and everyone is well especially your son who I suppose was thrilled at your return.

I am afraid my life is not going as well as I expected it to. We have been living with Jim's parents in a flat above a fish and chip shop and sleep in a small room next to his parents' bedroom. As the walls are thin you can hear every noise so you can imagine what I am talking about.

His mother treats me like a navvy as I am expected to do everything while she sits with her feet up or takes herself to bingo. His father seems to be some sort of crook as he has been in trouble with the law on a few occasions. The first time was when we had just arrived and two policemen turned up at the door asking questions about him. I think he has been selling stolen goods at the pub and goodness knows what else!

My pregnancy is progressing, and I have quite a prominent bump. The sickness I had earlier has gone which I am glad about as I do not think I could have withstood that as well as all the other things I am putting up with. Thankfully Jim was reinstated at the bank so I am hoping that we will be able to move somewhere else when our finances improve.

We visited my parents the day after we moved into the "shop." Mother was quite taken aback as I knew she would be. It must have been a shock for her to meet her only daughter at the door married and pregnant to an ex-soldier cum bank teller. She always had hopes that I would marry a doctor and walk down the aisle in a vision of white. Father, however, took the news in his stride even pouring out whisky to wish us well.

I am sorry to unburden myself like this but presently you are the only person I can confide in as I have been unable yet to make any friends and I dare not let my parents know what is going on.

Please write to me when you have a chance as I really valued our friendship on the Nea Hellas.

Sincerely,

Meg.

She could not bring herself to mention how Jim treated her as Helen had warned her about "marrying in haste and repenting at leisure." How true that had become she thought sealing the envelope and affixing the stamp however, what was done was done and all she could do was hope that things would improve. In one of his better post coital moods Jim had intimated there was a chance they might be able to move out of his parents' place and into a place of their own albeit a small one. It had been music to her ears. She would not care if it was a shoebox as long as they weren't sharing with people like his parents. Oh, to have a kitchen to herself, to have their meals at whatever time they wanted, not like now when there was some sort of meal shift going on and she and Jim waiting until her mother-in-law served up her dinner.

She grabbed her coat and shutting the door made her way gingerly down the stairs, the greasy fumes emanating from the shop becoming stronger with every step. She would never get used to the smell which permeated every nook and cranny tainting the curtains and even their bed. Nor would she get used to the stench of the tobacco or the ash from her mother in law's cigarette falling into whatever she was cooking. "Bit of ash don't hurt nobody," she had told Meg who alerted her when she noticed Maud mixing it in with the flour and eggs. Meanwhile her father-in-law leered at her with his beer-soaked eyes and sausage hands she had to fend off on more than one occasion, her pregnancy seemingly no deterrence.

Her dream of having their own accommodation was shattered when Jim announced they would be relocating to a guest house in Brighton.

"But I thought you said we would have our own place," sobbed Meg as she stuffed her underwear into a bag.

"Well, it didn't work out. All the houses are too expensive for the likes of us. I was counting on getting a raise but the powers that be had second thoughts."

"How long will we have to stay there?" And what about when the baby comes, how will we all fit into one room?"

"Bloody hell," he shouted. "Will you stop with the fucking questions!" "We'll deal with that when the kid arrives. Now hurry up with the packing. Herbie will be here soon to give us a lift."

He stormed out of the room.

Meg wiped away tears and threw her shoes into the suitcase. Oh,

God, what would become of her now? She knew that when the baby came, they would be evicted as no guest house was going to tolerate a screaming infant disturbing the other occupants. And why on earth were they going to Brighton, a million miles from here? Surely there would be some place closer than that. He would have to commute from there to the bank which would mean catching an early train and lord knows how late he would be returning home. Her mind swirled with questions which she would keep to herself as lately Jim's behaviour was volatile. She still had a sore arm which he had twisted because she had not ironed his shirt to his satisfaction.

Surrounded by detritus and a few stray cats, the dirty brown edifice rearing drunkenly by the promenade was worse than Meg could have envisaged. The wizened landlady who showed them in reminded Meg of a witch who only needed a broomstick to complete the picture.

"How long you got dearie?" she asked Meg glancing at her protuberant stomach.

"Oh, about three months I think," replied Meg unsure of her reply.

"Well, we'll see how we go when it's here. If it don't scream all night, I might make allowances. There was a girl staying here before with a kid who didn't give no trouble, so she was lucky to stay on. I can't have my other guests disturbed now, can I?"

After the rental transaction had been dealt with which turned out to be thirty bob a week for a double room, Meg followed Jim and trudged up the creaking stairs to the third floor. A malodorous smell assailed her. It was redolent of stale tobacco, cabbage and other indeterminate odours akin to unwashed bodies. Would ghastly smells follow her the rest of her life? On the second floor, a door opened to reveal a spectral hand depositing a pile of food on the carpet leaving Meg to wonder if she really witnessed that or were hallucinations becoming another burden with which she would have to deal.

Chapter Twelve

As the weeks continued Meg knew what a grave error, she had made coercing Jim into marrying her. In his estimation she was in his words, "a worthless piece of shit" unable to do anything right which behaviour he felt warranted a good slap around the face or elsewhere. He suspected her of flirting with one of the lodgers, a morose Greek named Nikos who had lost his wife and child in the war and was now confined to this single cell of a room scraping a living as a waiter in the restaurant on the pier. Jim had seen her one day engaged in conversation Meg desperate to hear about the country she had left behind in the vain hope that this waiter would know someone who knew something of her lover, Stavros. Nikos was unable to shed any light on the whereabouts of Stavros, instead regaling her with his experiences as a waiter especially in one of the Brasseries in Paris. He told her how the waiters stole each other's tips, the rats as big as cats scurrying around the wine cellar, the night he helped another waiter pick up food from the dirty floor and returning it to the plate for delivery to the unwary customer, how the chief cook, a gargantuan Arab, had threatened him with a carving knife. He had lived in a squalid hotel sharing a room with a fellow who snored and farted all night then moved into a garret infested with bed bugs whose bites left him covered in itchy welts. He was perpetually tired and hungry only living on bread rolls and bitter coffee. Those experiences had been the reason he had fled the city of light and washed up here in Britain.

She initially befriended him when he had knocked on her door requesting her assistance for his finger which he had cut on a broken wine glass. He had been told by the landlady that she had been a nurse in the war and hoped she would be able to help him.

"Oh, I think you had better go to the doctor and have it stitched," she advised after ascertaining the damage.

"No, no, I cannot afford. Please, you do something?"

She gestured him inside and told him to sit meanwhile thanking God that Jim was at work and not here to see her ministering to this man with whom he would probably assume she was having an affair. She took from the cupboard her First Aid tin and extracted cotton wool, a bandage, and some iodine. She placed the contents on the table and drew up another chair to face him.

"Let's see if this does the job but I must warn you that if you don't have stitches, you will end up with a scar."

He replied about not caring about a scar as he had others and one more would not make a difference. Meg wondered where the others were and how they had come about. Were they from any other Arabs brandishing knives or were they a result of the war?

She decided to ask him.

"Did you get the scars in the war?"

"No, I was in Foreign Legion in North Africa," he replied. "Many bad men in Legion. Many running away from something."

"Did one of them attack you?"

He was reticent to answer instead asking her a question instead.

"How long?" Looking at her stomach.

"Only a few months," she replied winding the bandage around his finger then tying it off.

"There," she said, "all finished. Try to keep it dry." She handed him another bandage instructing him to change it in two days.

"Efharisto, thank you," he said as she escorted him to the door

"Endaxi, ok." She loved speaking Greek again and ministering to the waiter, applying her nursing skills just as she had done to Stavros in that cave in Chania. Oh, my Stavy, why did you have to leave me? Where are you now? It was her usual question, the usual refrain, the memory of him never be to be extinguished.

"Can't that fucker shut up?" Jim exploded one night a few weeks after she had tended to Nikos' finger. The thin walls allowed every sound to penetrate and, as the Greek's room was next to theirs, pots and pans could be heard clanking and banging as he cooked himself something after his late shift.

Jim leapt from the bed.

"What are you going to do?" cried Meg now sitting up worried about what might transpire.

"I'm going to have a word."

Terrified, Meg slunk down into the bed praying that no harm would befall that poor wretch next door.

She heard Jim banging on the door, his raised voice then silence.

He returned to bed.

"Shouldn't have any more trouble from him," he said, settling himself and pulling up the blanket.

"And" he added. "If you know what's good for you, you better stop your flirting. I know what you're up to."

Why was he so paranoid? Why did he think she was flirting especially in her condition with a pregnant stomach. It would not be further from her mind. She was too scared to defend herself and to ask him what he had said to Nikos. It was better being uncommunicative. That way she would not rile him if she said something with which he did not agree. That usually ended with her taking the brunt of his rages. The rest of the night Meg lay awake attuned to any noise which might be forthcoming, any sound which might again ignite her husband into another fury. However, all remained quiet until the alarm told them it was time to arise and greet another day in Brighton.

Chapter Thirteen

Many days had passed and there had been no sign of the Greek waiter which aroused Meg's concern. She determined to find out about his absence and accosted the landlady who was desultorily flicking a duster over the skirting boards.

"Your guess is as good as mine, ducks," she replied. "And if I see him again, he'll get a good piece of my mind. Took off without a by your leave, he did and owes me rent. His things are still in his room."

"Don't you think you should call the police?" asked Meg now thoroughly worried her mind reverting to what had transpired the night of the confrontation.

"Nah, he probably did a runner knowing he owed me rent. Had another one the same, Turkish I think he was. He owed me money. Took off gawd knows where. You can't trust these foreigners I tell you. They're a bad bunch and no mistake. Don't know why I let them in. Talking of rent," she added. "Yours is overdue. Make sure you tell that husband of yours when he comes home otherwise, I will have to have a word."

"Oh, oh, yes. I will tell him. It must have skipped his mind. He has been a bit busy at work."

"Make sure you do then. I'm not running a charity here."

She bustled off up the stairs stopping at the door on the second floor. The door from which Meg had noticed the hand placing the pile of food. She had caught sight of the mystery person a few days ago. A lank haired skinny vision with a deathly pallor who was in the process of trying to secrete more food behind the phone table. There seemed to be a familial resemblance to the landlady. Was she her daughter or some relative?

Her thoughts segued to the overdue rent. What was that about? Surely Jim was earning enough money at the bank? She would have to get him in a good mood to tell him. After she cooked his favourite shepherd's pie and maybe a bottle of ale. Or maybe not the ale as alcohol seemed to arouse his violent tendencies. Lately, he was going out after tea and returning reeking of it as well as tobacco hours later when she was in bed. She had ceased asking him where he went, the first time that resulted in a black eye. Was he seeing someone else someone who was not pregnant and could give him what he wanted? It would be a relief if he was having an affair instead of her having to be available for sex whenever and wherever he wanted. Surely, he was not using the rent money to pay a prostitute? She knew from the war men who had contracted all sorts of infections from those people, diseases which led to blindness, insanity and even still birth, the latter not bearing to be thought about. She continued berating herself, for becoming involved with him, coercing him into marriage. She would have been better off as an unwed mother residing with her parents. The stigma would have been more easily borne than the way she was living now, with an abuser and probably a philanderer as well. In his eyes she could not do anything to his liking. The more she tried the more he found fault with her. Maybe when the baby was born his moods would improve however, the way he and his father interacted there was not much chance of that. He was now incarcerated in Bellmarsh prison having been arrested for possession of stolen goods and the molestation of a child. When Meg had heard that she thanked God they were not still living over that fish and chip shop. Even this boarding house was better than residing with a child molester, her mind shredding at the thought of living there after her baby was born. It had been making its presence felt lately and she continued to be amazed at the way little lumps appeared on random areas of her stomach. Was it a foot, an elbow, or a heel? She showed Jim thinking he would be interested but the only comment he had was about the stretch marks which looked like little red veins, a sight he thought distasteful. She was glad that her pregnancy was progressing well, the local doctor assuring her that everything looked normal, the baby a good size.

In need of some air, she took herself and her thoughts out of the boarding house and commenced walking in the direction of the pier. It was a mild day with only a few wispy clouds scattered here and there, the pervasive seagulls swooping and diving with a few squabbling on the sand. She continued along the promenade past the tawdry facades, the paint stripped by the salty air, the iron railings rusted. It was only markedly better than the High Street where they lived before. The saving grace was the sea and the sand which always tended to improve her mood. She had loved going with her parents every year to Holkham beach in Norfolk where her father rented a cottage by the sea. She had loved the wildness of the place, the susurration of the sea grass, the beach devoid of people. The amiability of her parents towards each other which was not very evident at home in Putney. There would be picnics, walks along the beach, board games played at night in the glow of the lamps as the waves lapped softly outside the window. Her mother quietly knitting, her father with his pipe ensconced in a book. It was on the beach that she had decided to become a nurse, to minister to those in need of care, to try and relieve their suffering. She wondered why this place cast such a spell over them all and yearned for the day when her father could purchase the cottage and move there permanently. However, that did not eventuate and they returned to their suburban home in which quickly swirled the carping and acrimony, the snide remarks. She was at pains to understand it all. How the sea could instil such a change in someone's personality. Maybe it was because her father was on holiday, away from the stress and pressure of work. Her mother freed from the domestic routine, the mornings when she ensured that both her daughter and husband were fed a decent breakfast prior to leaving for school and work. The beach house also did not contain all the ephemera of their home, there were no religious icons on the walls, no dressers groaning with dusty bric- a- brac which Meg knew her father could not tolerate especially the items pertaining to the church.

Her walk had taken her to the pier where she sighted the restaurant, Bella Italia, the one where Nikos was employed. It was in the Casino complex. Should she go there and ask the management about the Greek waiter, if he had turned up for work? She had been plagued with curiosity and concern about his disappearance, especially as his belongings were still in his room. Approaching the Casino, she happened to look through one of the windows. To her astonishment, her eyes alighted on her husband at one of the roulette tables, a busty blonde whispering in his ear. My God, so this is where the rent money is going and on a week day, no less, when he should be at the Bank working! She felt faint and steadied herself leaning on the window to face the sea. How many days had he been doing this, dressed in his suit and tie pretending to catch the 7.30 train as she waved him off from the door, and how many nights? She changed her mind about visiting the restaurant. That would have to wait. What she needed now was a good strong cup of tea with sugar to settle her nerves. She slowly made her way back towards a café on the promenade her mind awash with the vision of Jim gambling with that tart, a divebombing seagull no deterrent to her thoughts. How dare he spend our money on gambling and hookers which was probably what that tart was in her low cut tight scarlet dress with lips to match!

She was just crossing the road when she noticed a newspaper boy brandishing the latest edition of The Brighton Herald. As she inched closer, she was assailed by his cry:" Extra, extra, read all about it! Body of Greek waiter discovered under Brighton pier."

Chapter Fourteen

At the end of that day on the pier, Jim arrived back at the boarding house, paid the landlady the overdue rent and told Meg to start packing as they would be leaving this "shit hole" for better accommodation. He had got lucky was his answer when she had questioned him about the sudden increase in finances, her mind's eye on that roulette table at which she had sighted him. She would never be able to tell him he had been spotted; the repercussions would be too great. She had not recovered from the shocks which had assailed her. The vision of him at the Casino with the tart and the realisation that the waiter was dead. Surely to God, Jim had nothing to do with that! The paper reported that the authorities opined it was a drowning or suicide which had caused his death, which was the usual verdict for types such as he, itinerant and poor, unworthy of a proper investigation. She had to cling onto that scenario, anything else could not be borne. "Get a move on," he yelled. "I've got a cab coming here in a minute."

Her heart beating wildly, she did as he requested, hurriedly packing bags as the baby made its presence felt kicking her here and there as though in protest against her anxiety. Her baby, Stavy's baby, would take priority above all else. She would do whatever it took to keep it safe. She would rather die than have any harm befall it. Then the usual mantra, oh, darling Stavy, why, why did you have to leave me?

The cab pulled up outside a rather upmarket hotel in Shoreham.

"Are we going to live here?" Meg tentatively asked as her eyes alighted on the impressive façade, the gleaming brass rails alongside the steps leading into the foyer.

"For a bit," he replied paying the driver and telling him to keep the change. He retrieved their luggage from the boot.

A uniformed doorman bustled over.

"Evening, sir, madam. Let me help you with your luggage."

Meg trailed after her husband into the foyer but hung back while he registered at the reception desk. She felt rather frumpy and out of place. She wished she had nicer clothes as her eyes alighted on the fine raiment of the guests surrounding her. Women in stylish dresses and hats, the slipstream of their perfume following in their wake. Their male companions garbed in tailored suits and ties.

"And how long might you be staying with us?" She heard the receptionist ask Jim who replied he was unsure but would let them know after a few nights. He must have won a lot of money in that Casino if they were to stay here in this place.

Only a few nights she heard him say. And where to after that? Would they be constantly changing addresses? She was so tired of this life, feeling like some sort of gypsy moving from place to place with no permanent home. Living in a grotty boarding house with all its insalubriousness. The tattered carpets, the creaking stairs, the shared scummy bath the drain in which contained stray hair both pubic, and otherwise. She could never have told Helen about her current situation and felt rather disappointed that she had not replied to her letter. Maybe it went to the wrong address, and she did not receive it. Maybe it was better she did not read it as now Meg was regretting having sent it. Helen's demeanour was quite refined, her husband was a doctor, her son in public school. What could I have been thinking that she would want to be associated with a type like me? She thought about the boarding house and the motley group of residents. At least there she had someone to talk to; the gossipy landlady, Doris who was always on for a chin wag, a kindly old retired army major, Harold, who always asked how she was inviting her into his room for a cup of tea and a custard cream. He always was good company, the two of them sharing their war time experiences. Meg was amazed to discover that his life had been saved by the Bible. In northeast France, in a trench he had been sleeping with his

Bible under his head. Without warning, a direct hit destroyed his dug-out almost completely, wounding and killing many of his comrades. Harold was unharmed and managed to extricate himself from the rubble. It was later when he retrieved his Bible, he discovered to his astonishment that the holy book had saved him as a piece of shrapnel tore the book under his head. He had shown Meg the precious memento, the torn Bible, his treasured souvenir from the French trench.

Down the hall, straight out of Great Expectations, garbed in a floor length satin gown and a lacy mantilla with rouged cheeks and matching overdrawn lips resided a ring-in for Miss Havisham. Doris had told Meg she was a long-term resident who had fallen on hard times and whose fiancée had died at the Somme. In a futile attempt to assuage her sorrow, she had taken to downing large amounts of gin or cheap sherry which accounted for her florid complexion. Cognisant of her own situation, Meg had complete empathy for this bereft woman, could understand the pain she was feeling. So, when she had invited Meg into her room one afternoon, she had accepted her invitation. Since it was after lunch, Meg thought there would be tea offered however, Miss Havisham (which was what Meg had named her) had staggered over to the bench and produced an opened bottle of London Dry Gin from which she poured two glasses.

"Oh," exclaimed Meg thoroughly startled. "I think it's a bit early in the day for me and, as you can see, I am expecting." Havisham patted her arm. "That's alright, dearie," she replied, hiccupping, the alcoholic fumes nearly making Meg gag." it means there's plenty more for me." Meg did not know how she could sit there and watch this poor woman disintegrate before her eyes. Surely there was something or someone who could assist and save her from a sure and painful death which was where she was headed. Doris had said she had scraped her off the footpath more than once as she returned from one of her nightly binges. Meg voiced her thoughts.

"I don't mean to be rude, but Doris told me about your drinking problem. You know there are places you can go to get help."

Havisham slammed down her glass. "Trust that bloody old bitch to tattle tale. She should keep her witch's nose out of my business. Always got something to gossip about. Pity she doesn't she fix up this dump instead of butting in where she's not wanted." Meg was taken aback by the outburst. She did not expect that reaction, the swearing, the enmity pouring forth from the vision in satin and lace. She had thought she was genteel not some sort of boorish creature. But then that is what alcohol does, when it is overly consumed, changing the victim's personality. The same thing had happened to her uncle, the drink turning him from a meek and mild gentleman into an aggressive wife beater, finally ending up in hospital dying of cirrhosis of the liver.

"I'm sorry I made you upset," said Meg. "I was just trying to help." Her hands sought her stomach as though to shield the baby from the tension, the inhalation of the alcoholic fumes permeating the space.

"You're as bad as her," she spluttered, poking a gnarly finger at Meg. "Sticking your nose into a body's business. Get out of here and leave me in peace." Meg scuttled out the door sorry for mentioning anything about the drinking. She was only trying to help the poor woman. But, as Doris had said, some people just don't want to be helped and if she did not want to leave the road to perdition then that was her problem. Meg could see her point but still felt sorry for being unable to do anything. Havisham was right about Doris being a busy body. She probably wondered about Jim and me. What was our story? She had tried to elicit information from Meg one morning after they had been there for three days as she was farewelling Jim. "Off to work, is he?"

"Yes."

"Where does he work then?"

"In a bank."

"Where's that, around here?"

"No, he works in London."

"Well, that's a good way from here. Can't he get a job closer?"

And on went the questions until Meg had to excuse herself to use the toilet. She could not really blame Doris for commenting about their circumstances especially when she found herself telling her they had previously been living with his parents above a fish and chip shop!

He could not seem to settle in one place, always on the move as though he was trying to escape from something or someone. Surely the war could not responsible for his attitude, his vacillating moods. He seemed so nice when she had encountered him on the ship not like the ogre he was now.

Jim was given the key and she followed him over to the lift which would take them to their room on the fifth floor. Nothing was said as they ascended. His taciturnity infusing the space like a miasma. She thought the silences were worse than the physical violence at least then there were words spoken albeit dripping with acrimony. She did not know how long she could tolerate the situation. Many nights would see her awake formulating a plan to leave him and return to her parents. However, his threats of killing her and the baby if she ever tried to leave him always prevented her from carrying out the scheme. Interspersed with those thoughts were her concerns for her Stavros. Was his marriage as unhappy as hers or had his wife mellowed with his absence? Did he again become a father? Would he want to know about the child he had seeded in that tenement on Alexandras Avenue? She pondered about whether she should tell him, but she did not know his correct address, just that it was a farm somewhere in the wilds of Perivolaki. Did he always think of her as she did him or had it been just a fleeting romance, two people thrown together in the maelstrom of war. However, she could not imagine it was that. Their love had been real, she was certain of it. They had a definite connection. It was not unrequited; his obeisance and amative words were surely proof of that.

Chapter Fifteen

Since that fateful day when he had said goodbye to his lover in Alexandras Avenue, Stavros devoted his time and energy to the farm. The work was plentiful as many people had left for the cities in search of jobs leaving the rural areas decimated. Dawn would see him up and out of bed where his wife lay snoring, mouth open, her face still lined with the scowls thrown at him during the day. How could she ever compare with Meg's beautiful smiling countenance, her raven tresses, that certain way she had of wrinkling her nose when she was querying something. He had sensed his wife knew about what he had been up to in the war, had known of his adulterous relationship in Athens, his mind always returning to that morning he had left her bereft at the door. He had been happy he had forgotten to take the dog tag; it would be something to remind her of him in the years to come. Ever since he had returned, his wife had shown a degree of reticence towards him, a suspicion that he was hiding something from her. He tried to rekindle some spark of what they had before he had left when there had been some modicum of love between them. That first night of his return he thought she would welcome his caresses, the nibbling of her ear which she used to like as a prelude to their lovemaking, but he was quickly rebuffed. She was too tired, worn out by all the work she had to do when he was away. And, more importantly, she did not want to have children as what was there to offer them here, what money did they have to support children, there was hardly enough for them to survive? So that was to be his life, he was to be punished for his indiscretions with no progeny either. He had been railroaded and coerced into the marriage, gullible enough to believe her story that she was pregnant, and the baby was his. However, no baby had eventuated her story being that it had come away from her one night in the latrine. She had been desperate to secure herself a husband to join those decorating the church with their bridal satin and confettied veils. He always thought he would have liked to have a son, a boy who would help him on the farm and maybe inherit it one day as he himself had inherited it from his father. He thought often of that man, his father, eking out a living on the Grecian soil slaking his thirst with glasses of Raki after a laborious day in the fields. He was a man replete with bonhomie humming bouzouki tunes, quite different from his timorous wife her hands constantly kneading the kombollois, sending supplications to the Lord for the welfare of her family and the continuing success of the farm. She was the one who instilled in her son all the values she held dear, the sedulous devotion to the Church to which she would drag Stavros every Sunday while his father slept soundly under the blankets recuperating from his Saturday night libations with the neighbours. He told his wife that his religion was with the animals he tended, the earth and the sky which always amazed him when the evening stars twinkled like precious jewels and the moon so close, he felt he could touch it. He had told Stavros about the constellation, the association to Greek mythology, about Orion who was a giant huntsman whom Zeus placed among the stars as the constellation of Orion. He told him names such as Andromeda, Aries, Aquarius, and others too plentiful to mention and Stavros had been entranced and proud of his father for being the fount of such wisdom. He had retained an amazement for the firmament when on cold clear nights he would sit in the field and gaze up at the shimmering jewels above him. It was in the maelstrom of the war when in the stasis of fighting he would look to the heavens, to Orion to feel acutely the presence of his parents, especially his father. His love of astronomy he had shared with Meg one clear night at the Acropolis when there had been a lull in the turmoil the rancorous mobs having moved on to other areas. Under the effulgence of a full moon, they had lain amidst the ancient ruins in the temple of Athena Parthenos (Athena the Virgin). That had brought forth some laughter, Meg whispering to Stavros what would Athena think of her now as she surrendered to his ardour. Their passion sated, Stavros then pointed out to her the various celestial bodies his father had shown him, all the Greek mythological names that he remembered. He had talked to her about his mother her devotion to the church and anything pertaining to religion. She had taken him once to a place called Agios Ioannis to which they had travelled on a weather paled old steamer filled with a motley collection of people, water jars, lemons, and goats. There had been pushing and shoving and quarrelling and complaining. They had followed an old woman with a black headscarf onto the boat her varicosed legs and rolled down stockings displayed from a flurry of black petticoats as she heaved herself aboard. She was holding by the claws a brace of docile looking fowls which Stavros thought to be dead as there had been no movement or noise emanating from them on the journey. He had enjoyed himself sucking some sticky sesame sweets, sitting beside his mother as the boat chugged along above the milky depths of the ocean. They arrived at the island his mother shepherding him off the boat then to embark on a steep climb to the apex where the Church and a convent were located. It was in the convent a terrifying sight had awaited him. It was a library of the skulls of dead nuns on white shelves decked with lace and he had hidden in the folds of his mother's dress while she made the sign of the cross and mumbled incantations to the collection before her. The vision of those skulls had ingrained itself into his mind never to be expunged. Meg was shocked that his mother had taken him, a young impressionable boy to see such a sight and thought of her own mother immersed in the same religion and if she would have done the same to her. Their time at the Acropolis was cut short as sounds became louder manifesting in some sort of mayhem down below and they scurried away down the cliff back to the safety and solace of their love nest in Alexandras Avenue.

Like his father, Stavros' time was spent in the fields, planting and harvesting before the heat of the day, before the caustic remarks of his wife had time to surface. He found the milking of the goats and especially the making of the cheese both satisfying and relaxing, the animals unable to render any antagonism towards him. He loved the feel of the teats in his hand the pressure releasing the warm milk into the bucket. Then after the processing of the cheese; the milk cooled; the rennet added to curdle the milk then the curd cut into small pieces to be heated in a pot to separate the liquid from the solids. The curds would be drained and pressed to remove any remaining whey then salted and allowed to age. At least they had a market for their produce, albeit a small one as their neighbours handed over a few drachma for the tasty morsels to be added to their salads and lamb. He was proud that he was able to produce such fine cheese, even crediting his wife for keeping the farm going so well while he was away. She, however, did not take well to those remarks thinking there was sarcasm lurking under the surface, some sort of hidden agenda.

He had accompanied her to celebrations mainly on feast days when his neighbours would invite them to partake of spit roasted lamb, spanakopita and salads to which Stavros would contribute his cheese. To the strains of the bouzouki, the raki would flow loosening the tongues, the inhibitions of the assembly as they tried to ward off their anxieties of the war and their future It was not long after the wedding she had solemnly and tearily announced that the baby had been lost. At the time he had believed her, had taken her into his arms and wiped away her tears of sorrow. However, as the marriage tottered along, he held suspicions. Had she really been carrying his child or was it just a ruse to marry him? There had been another woman in the village who had given him the glad eye, insinuating herself wherever he happened to be either in the Church, at the market or at one of the celebratory feasts. He had never encouraged her, always maintained his distance, remaining loyal to his wife. However, this night replete with raki and devoid of any guilt he had succumbed to her charms. What did he have to lose? He had already been disloyal in Chania and Athens, maybe this woman would assist him to assuage his feelings for Meg. At the very least it would relieve him of his sexual frustration and give him the body of a woman to feel and fuck.

His wife had left early that feast night, pleading a headache, the need to arise early in the morning which he knew was a lie as it was he who rose at dawn and not her. Fortified by liquor and devoid of inhibition, he was drawn towards the harlot, to her perfume which was redolent of the one Meg used to wear. It was called Midnight in Paris. He envisioned the little blue bottle on the table near their bed in their love nest in Athens. How she would dab a little behind her ears and between her breasts before they would come together in passion. Maybe he could pretend that this woman near him now was his lost love, Meg. He led her away from the gathering now well sated with lamb, the carcass of which lay on the rack, underneath the ashes smouldering, exuding a fatty lemony aroma. With nary a word spoken, he had taken her behind a gorse bush. Attempting to alleviate all the guilt, anger and tension accumulated since his return, he had driven into her forcefully so unlike how he used to be with Meg. Their lovemaking had always been slow and languid, taking their time to admire each other's bodies, to whisper loving words even amidst the ructions underneath their window, the marauding mobs.

It was after the illicit deed was completed, after she had rolled on her stockings and straightened her dress that she suggested another meeting. It would be a no strings attached situation she had said knowing he was married and seemingly loyal to his wife who was reputed to be the village harridan. He did not even know her name and did not care. It would be easier for her to remain unnamed, an anonymous receptacle into which he could deposit all his pent-up frustration. Was it the war which had made him like this? Someone who would callously exploit a woman in this way? However, she did not seem to be perturbed by the situation, acting like a whore, saying next time he could come to her house and she would indulge his fantasies, as she knew other sexual positions apart from the "missionary." That had piqued Stavros' interest, there was one position he always wanted to try, something his wife would not partake in, would not have been able to utter the word. Even Meg had not done that and he would not have expected her to. He had heard his comrades boast about their sexual exploits in the brothels about the different positions in which they had indulged. Maybe he would take up this woman's offer as what would he have to lose as he looked across at the lumpen body of his shrewish wife snoring beside him.

Chapter Sixteen

Abide with me, fast falls the eventide
The darkness deepens Lord, with me abide
When other helpers fail and comforts flee
Help of the helpless, oh, abide with me.

The words of the hymn brought tears to Theo's eyes. His darling mother who nurtured and cared for him, trying to shield him from his father's violence, who supported him in his sexual orientation, his wonderful travelling companion, a devoted and brave nurse who had stood up to the Germans, now lying dead in the coffin she requested. She had lingered on for four weeks during which time her mind traversed the landscape of her life. She did not know if all of it had happened or if it was the morphine administered at regular intervals. However, she always had an eidetic memory able to vividly recall whatever came to mind.

Visions arose of Germans and bombs, a cave in Chania, a wounded soldier, a room in Athens imbued with passionate love. On the high seas in a troop ship, a marriage, violence, a birth, prison, and death. She remembered clearly when her baby had been born, a beautiful son on whom her love was bestowed. Her Theo, Stavros' baby who would grow and become a son any mother would be proud of. She would have loved to have told Stavros that he had a son often wondering about him if his life had been happier than hers. She was grateful that Theo had not been unduly traumatised by the violence which had occurred, violence from which she had tried to shield him when he was a little boy. She could not tell anyone about what she was experiencing especially her parents. There were times when she found herself on the verge of saying something but the words could not be uttered. And then it was too late, they had been killed instantly her father attempting to overtake a truck on their way home from their favourite place in Holkham. Meg's devastation had been overwhelming when she had heard the news and it was a while until she fully recovered from the shock. She had attributed her recovery to her darling Theo, to his smiles and his baby babble, his little fingers stroking her face. It was impossible to remain in bed when he had to be bathed, fed, and cared for.

Meg had inherited the house in Putney which had to be put into some semblance of order before she, Jim and Theo moved in. Jim had been rather chuffed at the thought of that, vacating the rented flat in Camden and moving to a more genteel area. Camden had been where they moved after their stay in that hotel in Shoreham which had lasted a couple of weeks. Camden was an insalubrious area, not a nice place to bring up a child and Meg had also been glad to vacate it. Meg had not looked forward to the chore of sorting the house, her family home where she had spent her childhood until she had enlisted in the war. She had wanted to go to the house on her own without the presence of Jim who she knew would mock her mother's ephemera, her knick knacks. "What do you want these things for? They're just a lot of bloody junk." Jim had told her as she returned her mother's set of teaspoons to the drawer after polishing them and leaving the three toby jugs on the dresser. "No, they're not and they belonged to mum so I am going to keep them," replied Meg. She was glad when he had enough, deciding to take Theo outside for a walk. She knew where he would go, on a search for the nearest pub. "Leave bubby here with me, please" she said, not wanting her baby anywhere near such a place. "Ok, please yourself. Don't know how long I'll be as it's Saturday." She knew all about Saturday; the day when he immersed himself in the dart competitions, fuelled by copious libations, arriving home in a drunken stupor fist flailing demanding to be fed at the ungodly hour of 10.00pm. She hoped and prayed today would not be one of those days as she removed the religious icons from the walls placing them in a bag to be taken to the Catholic charity on the High Street. Sorry mum, she whispered as the Sacred Heart was taken down from over her bed to be dispatched into the bag her aversion to it still strong after all this time. She took a minute to sit on the bed covered by the pink chenille eiderdown of her childhood. Her eyes alighted on the bookcase her father had bought her from the flea market when she was twelve to house her collection of books. She walked over and retrieved one of them. It was titled Nurse which was one of her favourites instilling an early interest in things medical. Also on the bookcase was My Doll's Nursing Set, a present from Santa. It contained a tiny doll, a bell, and a bandage. Many hours she would spend in her pretend hospital as her doll would be bandaged and pretend medicine administered. How she had looked forward to Christmas, the excitement of Santa dashing across the night sky in his sleigh laden with presents. The leaving of the carrots for his reindeer, her awakening before dawn to see what Santa had left under the tree, her joyous exclamations waking her parents from their slumber. Then the Church service, the singing of Silent Night and Hark the Herald Angels Sing, the roast turkey and bread sauce, the plum pudding made by her mother then steamed in its muslin bag for hours. The jollity of pulling the bon- bons to reveal a sweet or trinket inside.

Those times had been happy and it was only when she was older, she noticed the underlying tension in the house, a simmering resentment between her parents. She closed the door of her room leaving it to its memories then tackled her parents' bedroom. She removed the crucifix over the bed then opened her mother's wardrobe which greeted her with the aroma of her mother's perfume, Yardley's English Lavendar. It seemed to permeate all her clothes. She pulled a dress off the hanger and sat on the floor with her nose pressed into its folds, her unchecked tears dampening the fabric. Oh mum, she sobbed. I wish you were still here, why did you and dad have to die? There was so much I wanted to tell you but I was afraid of what you would say. How could I tell you that I had lost my virginity to a soldier in Greece and became pregnant to him? What would you have said if I had told you that I coerced another man into marriage letting him think it was his baby in my stomach and not another man's? How this man turned out to be an evil, gambling wife beater who threatened to kill me and my baby if I ever left him? She did not know how long she had sat there until the cries of Theo alerted her to the present. That day had been replete with memories both good and bad as she had sorted her mother's things into some sort of order. A pile for charity, another to be discarded and another for keeping. It was when she had investigated her father's wardrobe, she had been rather astounded and puzzled for there, lurking in the back behind some old singlets and a holey jumper, was an assortment of lacy panties and bras. What on earth could they be doing there in her father's cupboard? She knew her mother did not wear such confections, her underwear was plain and practical. Surely, they weren't the property of a girlfriend? Were there any other things that her father had hidden away? Meg was determined to find out. She started pulling everything out; ties, shirts, underpants, singlets, socks, handkerchiefs all landing higgledy- piggledy on the floor.

Drawers were opened, the contents thrown onto the pile. There was nothing else of interest to be discovered. So, dad had a girlfriend, but why did he have her underwear in his cupboard, Meg puzzled. It did not make sense. Surely, the girl would not leave her things here for Meg's mother to discover. She would have them in her own place. Now too exhausted to continue with the sorting she commenced returning the items to their allotted places. She would deal with it all another day. As she placed some socks into the second drawer, her eyes were drawn to a tiny bulge underneath the newspaper lining which she had not noticed before. Could this be something he had secreted away? Slowly, she peeled back the lining unearthing three photos. She turned them over to discover to her absolute shock they were of her father dressed in a woman's heeled shoes, a bra and lacy panties bending over to receive a cane on his backside!

My God, dad, what on earth, who are you? Meg screamed, her shaking hands grasping the photos. It can't be you, it's too ridiculous, too shocking. She could not believe what she was seeing that her dad was some sort of queer person, a cross dresser. She had heard about such people but would not in a million years think her father would be one. How could he do that to mum? Please, God she would not have known that about you. It would have been the end for her knowing that her husband was into such a scandalous thing, a thing which would certainly condemn his soul to hell. Who took the photos and who was at the end of that cane, some prostitute? It did not bear thinking about. It was all too dreadful. She stuffed the incriminating photos and the women's underwear into a bag which she would throw into the closest incinerator she could find. She would never be able to tell a living soul, her father's secret would be taken with her to her grave. In the intervening years, she had ruminated about it. She and her father both had secrets, he with the cross dressing, she having a baby out of wedlock cuckolding another man into marriage letting him think it was his child. Maybe her father would have understood her predicament, would have had some sympathy for her. She would have had someone in whom to confide. She was sure he would have supported her when she had been trying to rear Theo alone on a social security pension as Jim served six years in Belmarsh prison, the same one in which his father was incarcerated. He had been arrested for forging cheques at the bank, the proceeds filling the coffers of bookmakers at the races and other gambling venues. She knew that had been the reason he had kept moving, changing addresses to keep one step ahead of the authorities. He had left the employ of the first bank under a cloud of suspicion which was when she had witnessed him gambling at the casino when he should have been at work. Although it had been hard knowing her husband was a criminal at least she had a respite from him, from his violence and abuse and Theo did not have to hear or witness it. She always suspected him of killing the poor Greek waiter, as he had been certainly capable of it.

She had summoned the courage to talk with a couple of the women, the mothers at Theo's school. She invented a story about her husband confined to a TB sanatorium for an indefinite time which was where Theo thought he was. The women all conveyed their sympathy towards her some even offering their prayers for his speedy recovery. She also prayed that they would not read about his criminal exploits in the newspaper as had been the case with his father's incarceration. However, their surname, Williams, was a common one so if anyone had asked, she would say she had no relation to him as her husband was in the sanitorium dying of TB. There had been only one occasion when she had visited the jail while Theo was in school. She had thought that he might have been mollified by his situation would be pleased to see a familiar face but his attitude towards her had been the same and she had fled the facility vowing never to return. It had been a blessing when his heart had failed freeing her and Theo to live their lives unencumbered. Free from the tension, the shame, the abuse, and violence. In her final fevered days, she had wanted to tell him but her shame precluded her. Would he want to know that his father was not that abusive criminal bastard but a sweet gentle man who had adored her? But what would he think of her, his mother whom he had revered, a woman impregnated by a Greek soldier who had coerced another man into marriage? No, like her father's secret she would die with it locked in her heart.

Now it was time for Theo to speak, to pay tribute to his beloved mother. He was grateful that Kevin was by his side to support him if he floundered, if his voice was halted by his anguish. He had his words written down, a compendium of what he would say to the small assembly in the Church. He would let each person there know how wonderful his mother was, a devoted nurse who endured all the many tribulations of the war, a brave woman who had stood up to the Germans who spared her life. A magnificent mother who had singlehandedly raised him to be a son to be proud of, an intrepid travelling companion who had accompanied him to Paris and Chania not long before this day. His voice faltered at the mention of Chania, the place where her ashes would be scattered into the sea. It brought home to him the finality of her, she would never more be around to converse with, to laugh at the things they both found humorous, their repartee, their private little jokes. He had ended the eulogy with a poem by Wordsworth which he thought was appropriate:

What though the radiance, which was once so bright
Be now forever taken from my sight,
Of splendour in the grass, of glory in the flower,
We will grieve not, rather find
Strength in what remains behind.

Chapter Seventeen

Mired in the depths of his sorrow, Theo only accepted wedding ceremonies as presently funerals were too hard for him to bear. He had barely coped with the eulogy, Kevin's arm around his shoulder championing, encouraging him on. He had been grateful that the weather had been fine as there was nothing worse than a funeral held in the rain, adding extra dolour to the dourness of the day. The sun his mother always loved, availing herself of it at every opportunity, taking him to the park to play on the swings or to the seaside when there was just her and him, his father no longer alive. A picnic would be packed, sandwiches and cake and a bottle of cordial and off they would set to catch the train to Chalkwell beach. It was his favourite outing, seated beside his beaming mother, the picnic basket at her feet, the bag containing towels, his bucket and spade as his eyes beheld the passing scenery, the various stations, the people alighting and boarding the train and then behold, the first glimpse of the sea! "How many more stations til we get off?" was the perennial question as soon as the sea hove into view. "Two more darling," would be the reply as her velvety hands caressed his head.

As soon as the train doors opened, off he would bolt ahead of her anxious to be on the sand and in the salty water. She would set up in the same location near the rockpools and take him to explore all the organisms living within, the tiny crabs, the periwinkles, the oysters clinging to the rock. He would always take home with him a few periwinkles and some shells which he would put to his ear listening to the sound of the sea. She would take him into the shallows teaching him to swim her arms underneath him, his little legs kicking as instructed then one day, no longer supported, he was on his own managing to stay afloat with only one mouthful of salt water ingested. He was unperturbed about his father dying of that disease called TB and even felt glad about it. He would not have to cringe any more when he heard the ructions, the screams of his mother. Through the years, he had ruminated why his mother had married such a man, what had attracted her to him in the first place? He had once questioned her about it to be given a reply that he had not always been that way, excusing his behaviour as result of the war.

Her ashes were now in an urn of which Kevin had taken charge secreting it in his side of the wardrobe until such time when Theo could deal with it. He had told Theo whenever he was ready that he would come with him to Chania. Hoping to divert him from his disconsolation,

Kevin had booked them for a weekend at the country hotel. However, even the grandiosity of the establishment had failed to lift his mood.

"I hate seeing you like this hon," said Kevin grasping Theo's hand over the table. They were having breakfast at a damask covered table by the quarter pane window looking out onto the manicured lawns, the fountain spraying cascades of water, the dew dropped hollyhocks and lavender vying for space with roses and delphiniums.

"Sorry I'm not better company," said Theo desultorily taking a bite of the marmalade toast thinking what a waste of a weekend it had been. They only made love once and that only to appease Kevin for his generosity in making the reservation.

"Do you think you had better see a doctor when we get back?" Kevin announced." Maybe you might need something to get you through this rough patch?"

"What, you mean antidepressants?"

"Well, yes, probably. I've heard they can be helpful in times like these."

"But I don't want to become addicted."

"No, you won't. You will probably only have to take them for a short while. Just get you over this hump."

Theo thought about it. He would have to do something about the situation. He could not continue like this. He was also having trouble sleeping, tossing, and turning and getting up in the wasteland of the night to watch inane programs on television attempting to divert himself from other more concerning things. Lately, he had noticed bruising appearing on various parts of his body which he had tried to keep hidden from Kevin he only commenting on one on his leg. Theo had told him he had probably knocked himself against something to allay any suspicion. However, now, alarmingly, he was having intermittent nose bleeds, the last occurring to his embarrassment just as he was pronouncing a couple husband and wife. What on earth was happening to him?

Chapter Eighteen

"And how long have had the bruising and the nose bleeds?" asked the doctor as Theo commenced dressing. He had already been given a prescription for some low dose antidepressants and sleeping tablets to temporarily assist him through the worst of his grief.

"A few weeks I guess," replied Theo.

"Come over and take a seat."

Theo did as the doctor ordered and sat across from him at the desk.

The doctor steepled his fingers.

"In my opinion, you could have what is known as Von Willebrand's disease."

"Oh, what on earth is that?"

"It is similar to haemophilia, a blood disorder. There is a protein lacking which plays a key role in clotting."

"Is it treatable?"

"Yes, up to a point. You can buy over the counter medications such as aspirin or ibuproven to prevent bleeding. There is also an injection called Desmopressin which is a synthetic hormone which seems to be beneficial in controlling bleeding."

"Are either of your parents Greek by any chance?" He asked.

"Greek?" No, no they were English. Why do you ask?"

"Well, Von Willebrand is an inherited disease passed down mainly through the Greek line."

Theo sat transfixed trying to take in what the doctor was saying. His parents Greek? That could not be right.

The doctor said, "I will give you a referral to a Haematologist to confirm my diagnosis." Theo watched him writing out a form and signing it. He handed it to Theo.

"This fellow practices in Harley Street so you might find it hard to obtain an early appointment. Now, I want to see you in a month's time to see how you are travelling with the medication I gave you and do not be too concerned with the disease. With careful management you can go on to lead a normal life."

They both stood up and Theo shook the doctor's hand. In a trance like state, he vacated the room. He felt disembodied hearing himself asking the receptionist for another appointment then stumbled out into the hustle of the crowd going about their everyday affairs. Normal life? How could his life ever be normal now he had this bloody disease? Living on aspirin and injections. He needed a drink to salve his worries before he had to take those antidepressants which the doctor had warned should not be taken with alcohol. He certainly needed some antidepressants now even if he did not before. He ambled along to the next corner where a hotel stood and joined the early imbibers at the bar.

"A scotch, thanks. On second thought, better make it a double." He said to the barman.

"Right, you are guv. Hard night, eh?"

"No, hard morning."

The barman gave no reply but turned his back to take from the shelf a bottle of Johnnie Walker from which he poured a good measure into a glass placing it on the counter in front of Theo.

"That'll be five pounds fifty, thanks sport."

Theo proferred his credit card which the barman swiped handing him the receipt.

He took the glass over to a vacant snug in the corner noticing as he walked the stickiness of the carpet clinging to his shoes. The hotel was not like the upmarket ones he frequented with Kevin. This one appeared to be more for the working-class types, the tradesmen, the people coming off night shift and other desperates like himself in need of an early drink. He placed the glass on the table which was also sticky along with indeterminate stains and scratches on the wood one of which he could make out as someone's initials with an arrow running through them and wondered if the engraver had also the same worries as he. He took another slurp of his drink the fire in his throat a distraction from the issue confronting him. What the devil did that doctor mean about his parents being Greek? He could not understand it. He was glad he did not have anything scheduled for today, no weddings or funerals especially the latter. His mind was in turmoil. How was he going to cope with this bloody disease and how long was he going to live? He looked through the grimy window just able to discern the activity outside, the suited business men briefcases in hand, mothers pushing babies in prams, an elderly woman with a walker, the usual spectrum of humanity on a weekday in suburban London. He took the referral from his pocket. He was to see a Doctor Gavin Barr, Haematologist, Wycombe Hall, 89 Harley Street, phone 7034 8181. Might as well ring now Theo thought taking his mobile and keying in the number.

"Hello,' said Theo after his call was answered. "I have just been given a referral by my GP and would like to make an appointment to see Doctor Barr."

The receptionist asked him his name, date of birth, his address, and the name of his GP then after a pause advised him that there was a cancellation next Tuesday at 11.30. and would he like to come then. Theo looked up his schedule and found that he would be free as he only had a funeral in the afternoon at 2.00pm.

"Yes, thank you. I can come then." He told the woman at the end of the phone.

So that is sorted he said to himself putting away his phone and taking another good slurp of his drink. He was beginning to feel a bit tiddly. Better get some food inside me he thought. All he had for breakfast was a piece of toast and coffee and that was three hours ago. He left the half empty glass on the table and walked over to the bar.

"Hi," he said to the barman "any chance of ordering some food?"

"No problem, guv. What you fancy?"

"What's on offer?"

"The usual, ploughman's, sausage n chips."

"I'll have the ploughman's, thanks."

"Right you are. I'll bring it over to you."

"Cheers, thank you."

Theo returned to the table pleased that no one had taken away his unfinished scotch.

He sat down and fingered the glass wondering what Kevin would be doing now. Probably up to his eyeballs with documents and briefs and engaging with clients in one of the conference rooms or conversing on the phone. He had promised Theo he would slow down a bit after the current case was completed but that had ended and now, he was embarking on a new matter which would again require his energy and attention. Theo worried that all the hard work would be detrimental to Kevin's health. Heaven forbid, that he died from a heart attack! Now Theo had been diagnosed with this disease it had put things into perspective. There was more to life than working. They could do without the gourmet food from Harrods, the dinner parties which Kevin was fond of hosting, cooking things from scratch. They even had a pasta machine through which Kevin would thread the flour which he had tenderly kneaded. There were also perfectly decent wines they could buy for half of what they were paying now. Even this Johnnie Walker was not so bad. It seemed that the more money you had the more you wanted or needed. He had watched a show on television once about the poor in Bangladesh. Although they were living cheek by jowl in squalor, they all seemed happy, the barefoot kids chasing each other around in the dirt their faces alight with joy and laughter. The women going about their chores talking to their neighbours, helping each other out. He thought about where he and Kevin lived and was unable to name any of the other residents. People kept to themselves not wanting to be involved with anyone else. It was a terrible indictment of London and was probably the same in all the other great cities of the world.

The barman arrived with his food.

"How much do I owe you?" asked Theo.

"Seven pounds, thanks guv."

Theo paid again with his card then popped a gherkin into his mouth followed by a piece of salami.

Chapter Nineteen

"Von Willebrand's disease, what the hell is that?" Kevin queried.

"Yes, I had never heard of it either," replied Theo.

They were having dinner at the end of the fateful day when Theo had been diagnosed.

"The GP might have got it wrong."

"Yes, maybe, hopefully. Guess I will just have to wait to see the specialist next week for confirmation."

"And that was mysterious him asking you about having Greek ancestry."

Theo had thought the same as something he had seen when he was cleaning out his mother's house seemed to deepen the mystery. He had unearthed his mother's old Red Cross nurse's uniform and within its folds lay a soldier's dog tag. Inscribed were the words:

NAME STAVROS POULOS

SERVICE NUMBER 100000352006

BLOOD GROUP O

He had sat there mystified with it in his hand. Who was this soldier, Stavros? And what was he to his mother, her boyfriend, her lover? He had gathered up the uniform with the tag and brought it home with him storing it away at the back of his wardrobe vowing to tell Kevin when it was appropriate.

"Um, about the ancestry thing," announced Theo thinking that now would be the time to tell Kevin about what he had discovered at his mother's.

"What about it?"

"Well, there is something I found at mum's when I was cleaning up."

"Oh, anything interesting?"

"Hang on, I'll go and get it."

Kevin sat back, glass in hand enjoying the strains of Hayden wafting around the room. He cast his eyes on the objets d'art which he had sourced on his travels before he had met Theo. He had gone to Africa, to the Serengeti where he joined a tour group sleeping in tents under the limitless sky, the sounds of the nocturnal animals piercing the night. He had seen and been amazed by the migration of thousands of wildebeests trampling theplains. Zebras and antelopes abounded along with giraffes and flocks of birds winging their way to distant horizons. It had been a catharsis, what he had needed, after the disastrous break up of his marriage when he had confessed to his wife that he was gay and had been living a lie. A terrible fracas ensued, she firing an enfilade of accusations about his mendacity, his outright deception. "Why did you marry me in the first place, you fucking worthless piece of shit?" she screamed her scarlet nails scratching his face. But he had no answer to give her as he was as confused as she. Bereft at the table, he had watched her run into the bedroom to grab his clothes which were then hurled over the balcony. He watched as his white linen shirts and a suit landed in the turbid gutter as the next-door neighbour surveyed the scene with curiosity. He had been mortified by the whole situation and wondered if he should not have confessed, should have just continued in the marriage having illicit sex whenever he could. He had occasionally visited the public conveniences where there was always some desperate like himself, lurking around the cubicles to indulge his need, to suck him off or even have intercourse. However, he thought those places distasteful and sordid and were prone to being raided by the police who were always on the look-out for queers and poofters. Evicted from the marital home, he had sought refuge in a hotel from which he had rung the office pleading illness, some sort of stomach bug and was grateful that it was Friday. He would need the weekend to gather his thoughts and decide what to tell his colleagues. He had always wondered if some of them had suspicions about him seeing through his pretence at being a happily married man. He had ensured that his wife's photo was displayed prominently on his desk, his finger always adorned by the gold wedding band. His wife's ring had been hurled at him on that fateful day, glancing off his eyebrow and landing forlornly in the plush pile of the carpet. After the divorce, it had been a dismal time in that studio apartment which he had leased. He had felt unanchored like a boat drifting over a rough sea with no compass to point him in the right direction. He had resorted to pills and alcohol to numb his pain to induce the sleep which he craved. He took on more cases, throwing himself into the sanctum of the law, his weekends sinking into the mire of affidavits and briefs. His colleagues showed their concern especially the ones who had experienced divorce and its aftermath. "Plenty more where she came from sport," was the usual platitude as blind dates were offered and invitations to parties abounded. He had always pleaded disinterest. He needed time to lick his wounds, to regain some modicum of stability but thanked them all the same. How on earth could he tell them that he was gay and only interested in men?

He now looked across at the Makonde lion carving atop the piano which summoned the memory of the close encounter he had with that king of the jungle. He had loved the Masai in their colourful raiment of bright reds and whites, the women's necks adorned with myriad beads. They all had a happy countenance laughing and dancing and he thought about Theo's observation that people with little wealth seemed to be more contented and happier than others. Maybe there was some truth to that. There was more to life than amassing loads of money. However, he would find it hard to leave and live somewhere else. He had the impression that Theo wanted them to move to leave

London, to scale down their rather profligate lifestyle, and reign in the dinner parties. However, he loved to cook especially for other people. He found it relaxing. It took his mind off work and any other worries lurking in his mind such as his estrangement from his parents. He thought of poor Theo, contracting this awful disease. Surely that doctor was wrong. These doctors were not infallible. They made mistakes all the time.

His reverie was interrupted by Theo entering the room.

"What took you so long?"

"Had to go to the loo," he replied plonking himself on the chair next to Kevin with what resembled white material.

"Ok, I wondered where you had got to. Is this what you found at your mum's?" Kevin asked his eyes alighting on the item in Theo's hands.

"Yes, it's her Red Cross uniform."

"Ok, but what's that got to do with what we were talking about earlier?"

"It's what is wrapped up inside."

Theo unwrapped the uniform to display the dog tag.

"It's this, this dog tag. See, look, it belonged to a soldier called Stavros Poulos, which is certainly a Greek name," said Theo pointing out the inscription to Kevin.

"Ok, but it could have belonged to anyone. She could have found it in the war and kept it as a souvenir."

"Yes, she could have but I think there might be more to it than that."

"What, you mean he was her lover?"

"Exactly. And, more to the point, what if, what if, I am his son?"

"What? That's drawing rather a long bow, darl."

"Well, why not? It certainly would explain the Greek ancestry connection."

"Well, I wonder why she didn't tell you about him?"

"Probably because she was ashamed, I would think less of her. Think she was some sort of tart. We know that sort of behaviour was rather frowned upon in those days."

"Ok, so what do we do now?" Are you going to try and track this fellow down?" And where would you start? He might even be dead by now and even if he isn't, are you going to blurt out to him that you think he is your father? That could finish him off."

Theo sat there holding the precious bundle as tears welled and he started to cry until he was racked with sobs.

"It's going to be alright, my pet," said Kevin as he held him close allowing his lover to expunge his grief and shock.

"It's all been too much for you, the diagnosis and now this. Don't get all upset, I will try and do all I can to help you find him, if that is what you want."

"I must find him, Kev, if he is my father, before it's too late," gulped Theo through his sobs.

"Then that is what we will do. The two of us will team up and become a pair of sleuths."

Theo wiped his eyes and blew his nose.

"You know, it would be a relief if he is my actual father. I hated my dad, he was such a bastard."

Kevin knew about some of the violence Theo had experienced as a child. It had been one night not long after Theo had moved in with him that the nightmares descended waking them both with Theo's cries. Over glasses of brandy, they had sat up until the first light of dawn as Theo poured out his heart about what he and his mother had endured at the hands of his father. The beatings, the drunkenness, the coercive control of his mother which he now realised that is what it had been as his mother was devoid of friends.

"Have you had any more bleeding? "Kevin asked attempting to change the subject.

"No, thank God. Not since that wedding."

"Maybe it is settling down and you are on some sort of remission."

"Oh, God, wouldn't that be great?" I couldn't go through what I experienced at the dentist when they thought the bleeding would never stop. It was terrible."

Kevin moved up closer to Theo putting his arm around him in a gesture of comfort.

"Poor old thing," he said kissing his cheek.

"Thanks, appreciate it."

"I only wish there was something more I could for you. I hate to see you going through this."

Kevin turned and poured more wine into their glasses. It was another bottle of expensive cabernet sauvignon from

Calabria to pair with the fillet steak Kevin had cooked to perfection.

Theo thought about what he had been thinking in the pub this morning.

“Have you thought any more about slowing down?” He asked.

“That might go a long way in helping me. You know I worry about you and, we don’t need to be so extravagant. To be honest, I would be quite happy with a less expensive wine than this one and maybe a cheaper cut of meat.”

“What’s brought all this on darl?” Is it because of your diagnosis?”

“Yes, I suppose it has put everything into perspective.”

“If it’s going to make you feel better,” replied Kevin. “I will put some thought into what you just said but it will be hard renouncing a full-bodied red such as this,” as he swallowed the final drop of red, a feigned look of ecstasy washing across his face.

Chapter Twenty

It had been weeks since Theo had consulted Dr Barr who had given him a thorough examination and plied him with questions about his medical history, particularly if one of his parents had been Greek. That same question he had been asked by the GP, the thought which continually dogged his mind that the dog tag belonged to his father, his actual father who was from Greece! There had been numerous blood tests and genetic testing which all had confirmed the GP's diagnosis. Theo did indeed have von Willebrand's disease.

He was started on DDAVP, desmopressin to increase the von Willebrand factor levels and if his condition became severe, he would have to take antifibrinolytic drugs to prevent the breakdown of blood clots to control bleeding episodes. He was advised against taking aspirin and ensure he maintained good oral hygiene to minimise any bleeding of the gums. He was also advised not to participate in any activity which might increase the risk of injury. That was something he would not have to concerned about as he had never been interested in strenuous exercise, lifting weights at the gym or jogging. Unlike Kevin, who was up before dawn lacing up his runners to pound the pavement while Theo remained cosily cocooned under the doonah.

Today however, he was out of bed when Kevin returned from his run. They were expecting a phone call from the Greek Department of Defence who Kevin had contacted in an attempt to locate the whereabouts of one Stavros Poulos, soldier.

"I'm dying to know what they will say," called out Theo slurping his coffee.

"I was awake half the night wondering about it."

Kevin called back from the shower,

"Don't raise your hopes too much darl. I think this will be rather a mission impossible."

Theo fingered his eyebrow which he had been doing a lot lately, the stress overtaking him, the impatience to find his father all consuming.

At least he had not had any more bleeding episodes, the desmopressin was apparently working. He wished he could sleep better. His nights were filled with the overarching thoughts of the soldier. Was he actually his biological father? Was he alive or dead? If he was his father, he prayed that he was still alive and that he would find him before it was all too late. His supplications were offered in chapels and Churches before or after weddings and funerals. He prayed to Saint Anthony, patron saint of recovery of lost things, to Saint Jude, the help of the hopeless. He prayed before he lay down at night and when he lay awake watching the digital clock click by the minutes and the hours. When he did manage to sleep, he was consumed with scenes of war, of bombs, his father lying dead in a trench, the bloodied dog tag around his neck. He would wake in a scream and was pleased he had his lover beside him to offer him solace with kind words and coax him back to sleep.

Kevin now dressed was pouring his coffee when the phone rang.

"Oh, God, it's them," said Theo.

"Fingers crossed," replied Kevin before he picked up the phone.

Theo sat listening to what Kevin was saying.

"Yes, yes, I see. Well thank you for your assistance."

"What did they say? Do they know anything, do they know where he is?" asked Theo his words tumbling from his mouth as Kevin returned to the kitchen.

"Sorry old thing," said Kevin sitting down next to Theo and placing his arm around him feeling the tension in his shoulder.

"The only information they have is what we already know. Essentially, what is written on the dog tag and that he served as a soldier in the Second World War."

"Oh, I knew that's what would happen. I just knew it. Now we are back to square one."

Kevin took Theo's hands in his.

“Now, now, don’t worry. We still have another string to our bow.”

“Oh, what?”

“That private detective I told you about.”

“But I thought you said he was unavailable.”

“Actually, I rang him again yesterday. I wanted to talk with that defence department this morning to see what they had to offer, and I didn’t want to raise your hopes.”

“Oh, ok. What did he say? Is he available to help us now?”

“Yes, as a matter of fact, he is.”

“Oh, that’s great then. Can you contact him today?” Theo asked enthusiastically.

“Yes, when I get to the office which is where I should be now.”

He gave Theo a kiss, rinsed his coffee mug in the sink and grabbed his briefcase.

Theo walked to the door and held it open which was something he always did if he was around when Kevin departed.

“Have a good day, darl,” said Kevin planting a second kiss on Theo’s lips.

“You too and hope you get hold of that guy. He might be our saviour.”

Theo closed the door and made himself another coffee. He had the morning free until 1.00pm when he was to officiate at a funeral for an elderly gentleman who had passed at the age of 98. Living alone and alienated from his family, he had fallen and knocked his head, his body discovered by the police who had been alerted by one of his neighbours who had noticed a foul smell emanating from his flat. When the police had gained access, they had been confronted by a body in a bad state of decomposition, the buzzing of the flies signalling the man had been dead for some time. His neighbours had been shocked that they had been unaware of his plight as he tended to be rather a hermit, not emerging for days at a time. However, they had rallied to his cause donating whatever money they could spare to organise a farewell for him. Theo was also part of the cause, offering his time and not accepting any recompense for his service. This poor man could have been his father dying alone, to rot away without any family around him. Oh, God, please let him still be alive so I can see him and hold his hand. He sipped his coffee, his mind now segueing to that private detective whom Kevin managed to locate through the legal fraternity. At least he was Greek which he thought would be helpful speaking in the same dialect as he navigated the Greek system. How on earth would he be able to find his father? Where would he start? If he was a detective, he must know how to go about such things and Kevin had told him he had tracked down someone's relative who had been missing for years. He wondered if Kevin had managed to speak with him yet or was he immersed in the usual plethora of affidavits and depositions piled on his desk.

He finished his coffee then withdrew from his pocket the small eulogy he had written for the upcoming funeral. He had consulted the neighbours to glean what he could about the man's history and had discovered that he had served in the Second World War and had worked on the infamous Burma railway as a prisoner of the Japanese. Due to the maltreatment of his captors, he had turned to drink to assuage the terrible trauma and the unspeakable suffering he had endured. Bearing the brunt of his violence and mood disorders, his wife had left him taking the children with her.

Theo knew that the mourners would only comprise of the five neighbours, the funeral director and himself. It would be the first funeral of this size at which he had officiated. Most funerals had at least forty people, depending on the age of the deceased as the older one got the less friends there were. His mother's funeral was small as most of her friends had predeceased her leaving only fifteen mourners including himself and Kevin and some of their friends who had known his mother. Some of the attendees were nurses with whom Meg worked at the hospital. She had managed to secure casual employment there while Theo was at school, the money supplementing what she received from the government keeping them clothed and fed.

He read the words he would speak; how Albert served his country and endured unspeakable torture in a foreign land. He was due every honour and respect which you his kind neighbours have bequeathed to him. May we all acknowledge and thank Albert for his bravery and service for without that we would not be gathered here together in this free and democratic country. Go in peace Albert, and may the next life give you the solace you so rightly deserve. Theo thought what he had written was appropriate. He did not want to mention anything about his family who would not be present at the service.

He arrived at 1.50pm just before the assembly. A disparate group of shiny suited men with ties, three housewives garbed in their Sunday finery with feathered hats and strings of beads. They were all dressed to honour and respect Albert, their neighbour who lay in the plain plywood coffin, a posy of daffodils, Albert's favourite flower resting on top.

They all had listened intently to the eulogy, to Theo's words, as tissues found their way to eyes wet with tears.

Then, pressing the PLAY button on the portable cassette player he had brought, the hymn, BE NOT AFRAID resounded around the chapel:

You shall cross the barren desert,
But you shall not die of thirst.
You shall wander far in safety
Though you do not know the way.
You shall speak your words in foreign lands
And all will understand.
You shall see the face of God and live.
Be not afraid.

I go before you always.
Come follow, me, and I will give you rest.
If you pass through raging waters in the sea,
you shall not drown.
If you walk amid the burning flames,
you shall not be harmed.
If you stand before the pow'r of hell
and death is at your side,
know that I am with you through it all.
Be not afraid.
I go before you always.
Come, follow me, and I will give you rest.

The service now ended, Theo was thanked profusely for the giving of his time, his kind words of which they thought Albert would have approved and especially the hymn which did not leave a dry eye in the place. He was invited to partake of sandwiches and tea at Dulcie's flat, the lady with the church bazaar hair adorned with a fascinator which would not look out of place at Ascot. She had told him she had adopted Albert's parrot which the police had found when they had discovered the corpse. However, she was finding it quite hard as "cocky" would not stop screeching, "where's Albert?" continually on a loop throughout the day. Theo could not offer any advice except to try and communicate with the poor bird as much as she could and give him extra seed and maybe a toy to distract him. He had to decline her offer of refreshments due to a headache which threatened to evolve into a fully- fledged migraine. He noticed they were becoming more frequent lately. It was one of the effects of the disease. All he wanted now was to go home, take some Tylenol and sleep in a dark room.

Chapter Twenty-One

The weeks went inexorably on with no word from the detective, Nikos. The last they had heard was he had exhausted all avenues of enquiry in Greece. He had contacted all relevant authorities, including electoral rolls and local municipal councils but none of them had any information regarding a Stavros Poulos. Theo had all but given up any hope of his father being found, and he was resigning himself to the idea that he had probably died years before and was buried in some anonymous grave in the wilds of Greece.

"Don't give up hope, darl," said Kevin looking at Theo whose despondency exuded from his every pore. They were relaxing on the settee with the Sunday papers which all seemed to contain bad news about the economy or some member of parliament sexually harassing one of his colleagues. Tiddles, Meg's cat who they had adopted after her death, was curled up on the window ledge the rays of sunshine coaxing him to sleep.

"Where's Albert?" screeched cocky from his cage in the kitchen. He was now residing with them as Theo had contacted Dulcie a few weeks after the funeral enquiring how she was managing. He had felt so sorry for the wretched bird deprived of the only owner he had known and many a night would see him wondering about his welfare. Dulcie had told him she was at her wits' end with his screeching, and he had bitten her a few times for good measure. "I don't think he likes women, dear," she said to Theo when he arrived to take possession of him and his cage. "You're probably right Dulcie," replied Theo. "I hope he will be ok with us. At least we are both males."

Kevin was unsure about keeping the bird when Theo told him of his plan. "What about Tiddles?" he had asked.

"What about him?"

"Well, he might attack it if it flies out of the cage."

Don't worry. His wings are clipped. He can't fly anywhere."

"Well, what about the mess he will make? I hope you don't think I am going to clean it up."

"No, it will be my responsibility."

"Well, I will hold it to you."

Theo had kept his word sweeping and vacuuming the plethora of seeds which fell to the floor on a regular basis almost as regular as cocky's refrain. The only time he ceased was at night when the cover was placed over the cage.

"Isn't there some sort of sedative we can give him?" asked Kevin pouring over an Affidavit. "I can hardly concentrate."

"I'll find out. There's a vet clinic not far from the Church. I'll call in there after the wedding."

"Alright and ask them why he's pulling out his feathers."

Kevin returned to his document wishing that Theo had never set eyes on the bloody bird with its noisy screeching and its seeds littering the kitchen floor. Theo did his best to clean them up but there were always some he missed, hiding in crevices to sneakily re appear and be crunched under one's shoe. Kevin also disliked the appearance of the kitchen, the huge cage next to the French fridge totally disrupting the clean lines of the room. He also thought the bird harboured an animosity towards him staring at him with his malevolent eye whenever he was at the work bench preparing a meal and biting his finger when once he had poked it in the cage. There was no malevolence exhibited to Theo whenever he allowed the bird to perch on his shoulder and Kevin wondered why this was so. Was it that Theo reminded the bird of his owner, Albert? Now, as well as pulling out his feathers he had started pecking at his chest causing it to bleed, which Kevin thought was due to stress. The bird was nothing but trouble and really needed to be put out of its miserable existence. Kevin was reluctant to accost Theo about his perturbations as he knew it would end up in a row. Theo worshipped at the cult of sensitivity and could not abide any sort of contretemps or disturbance of the peace which was probably due to his childhood trauma. As his health issues were also a concern, Kevin would have to resort to biting his tongue and hope the bird would expire of natural causes sooner rather than later.

"I'm trying to stay positive, Kev," Theo now replied to Kevin's question. "But I wish we would hear something. It's been weeks now. I hope he hasn't given up on us."

"No, he hasn't. He's probably following up some leads and does not want to tell us anything until he has something positive to say."

"God, I hope so, I can't stand the suspense. I'd rather know one way or the other."

"Did you finish tidying up your mum's? "Kevin asked, steering Theo away from his present concern.

"Yes, for now."

Theo had spent time at his mother's house going through her possessions, sorting what was to be kept, thrown out or sent to the charity shops. Kevin had offered to go with him to help him with the task, but he declined his offer. He wanted to do it on his own. He thought it was a private thing, just him and his mother, just as they had always been, the two comrades in arms weathering the storm. He had tackled the wardrobe first his eyes scanning her dresses one in particular an old navy and white striped shirtmaker which she had seemed to favour wearing it more often than the others. He had thought it suited her so well especially when her hair was tied back with a yellow ribbon, his pride overflowing when she collected him from school thinking she was the most beautiful mother there. How could he consign this dress to the charity bag when it held such happy memories? He decided to keep it along with the uniform and the tag. Another dress caught his eye. This one, however did not evoke anything resembling happiness as it had borne the brunt of his father's rage, the material ripped at the front by his pugnacity. Theo tore it from the hanger and stuffed it into the throw out bag his ire raised at the thought of his mother being assaulted by that monster she married. He was puzzled why she would keep it, why it had not been relegated to the rubbish. However, she was not one who threw things out. Her philosophy had been to make do, mend and wear again. Well, that dress certainly had not been mended and had not been worn again. The remainder of her clothes he put into the charity bag along with her shoes. Next, he went to the chest of drawers unearthing her underwear, her bras, slips and panties, old suspender belts and stockings everything emitting an aroma which came from two lavender sachets secreted within the folds. She had a penchant for lavender in her twilight years as seemed to be the want of elderly women and he wondered why that was so. When he was a child, his mother had smelt of some other perfume, something more exotic and he wanted to find out what it was. Maybe he would discover an old bottle lurking around in the bathroom which was yet to be addressed. He extricated all the contents from the drawers and placed them in the charity bag which was now half filled.

He had hoped he would discover something she had hidden away like a love letter or a photo of her and Stavros. Something to prove that he had been her lover and Theo's father. He had however, found things belonging to him, her son, her baby. In a drawer, wrapped in tissue paper was enclosed a tiny nightdress, and a pair of blue knitted booties. Theo looked at them in wonder, in amazement at the size of them and was in disbelief that he could have been that tiny. He gathered them up and placed them in the bag he would take home to be treasured along with her nurse's uniform and the dog tag. In the hall cupboard he discovered his bucket and spade, evoking memories of those halcyon days at the beach. His battered, chewed stuffed rabbit which comforted him at night especially when the ructions were swirling. There were two matchbox cars, a tonka truck and an assortment of leggo bricks from which he would build various shapes to be knocked down and rebuilt numerous times.

However, his preference seemed to have been his mother's shoes, the heeled ones in which he would totter around when his father was absent to avoid the wrath he would incur especially if there was lipstick involved. There were his drawings, his attempts at cartoons drawn with his infant hand, of sausage men being chased with forks and bottles of tomato sauce. He tried to think what age he would have been then. Probably five or six he estimated.

How wonderful was it that his mother had kept his things. He wondered if Kevin's mother had done the same with his possessions. If when the time came for him to clean out his parents' house would he discover all the memorabilia belonging to his childhood as Theo had done? He wished Kevin could reconcile with his parents but according to Kevin, too much water had flowed under the bridge for there to be a reconnection. He intuited that his mother still harboured a vestige of rapprochement she having sent the musical Christmas cards. It had been his father who had banished him calling him a degenerate poofter with a warning never to set foot into the family home again until he came to his senses and renounced his debased life. After Kevin's divorce his father had suggested he undergo conversion therapy thinking that would set him on the righteous path of masculinity. Kevin had heard about this treatment involving electric shocks and paralysis inducing drugs which were completely ineffective in changing people's sexual orientation. He had met a fellow who had undergone this horrific therapy. It had left him permanently paralysed from the waist down, to spend the rest of his miserable life in a wheelchair.

"What do you feel like doing today?" now asked Kevin looking across at Theo who was immersed in the travel section. He was reading an article about Greece, the various bars and restaurants to visit, the places of interest such as the Acropolis and Knossos Palace. He wished he had not read it as his mind was brought again to Stavros who had not been located. Oh, God, where was he?

"Did you hear me, darl?"

"Oh, sorry, what did you say?"

"I asked you what you felt like doing today?"

"Oh, I'm easy." Theo replied, averting his face from the paper to turn his attention to his lover.

"Maybe we can have lunch at the Tate. They have a new exhibition," said Kevin.

"Oh, what is it?"

"The Rossettis."

"Ok, sounds perfect. We haven't been there for awhile, not since we saw John Sargent."

They had visited the Tate and other galleries on various weekends, their mutual interest in the arts confirmed on their first date over tapas and chablis in a dingy bar in Covent Garden. Theo had been pleased that he would have someone to accompany him as up until he met Kevin he usually went alone or with his mother, his other boy-friends disinterested in anything artistic. Meg had been responsible for his interest in the arts, the paintings by the grand masters such as Rembrandt, Rubens and his favourite impressionist, Van Gogh. When he was young, she would take him to the London Art Gallery and point out to him all the famous works exhibited there. However, his favourite time was in the café where he was treated to cake and lemonade as his mother sipped her English Breakfast tea, some sort of faraway look planted on her face. She had also bestowed on him a love of literature as visits to the library were undertaken where books were borrowed to be read and enjoyed especially at night under his blanket with his torch for light. Kevin had also indulged in this pursuit however he had been chastised by his mother, his torch and book confiscated. However, it had not diminished his love of the written word as the large bookcase in the sitting room was testament to that. On the shelves, among the Torts and Statutes, new and second-hand books jostled for space.

Tiddles leapt off the window ledge and padded over to the settee to purr around Theo's foot.

"You a good puss?" Theo said reaching down and stroking his fur which was soft against his skin. He was pleased that he had now settled down with them. It had taken him a while to become used to his new surroundings and the absence of Meg with whom he had been for many years. When they had brought him here, he had been off his food, fretting about his owner's absence. Gradually he had succumbed to his new owners' love and attention and being allowed to sleep at the end of their bed which was something until now, he had not been permitted to do. Theo's thoughts segued to his mother to her ashes which he now knew were secreted in Kevin's cupboard and wondered how long it would be until he would be able to cast his eyes on the urn, to hold it in his hands and disperse her remains into that sea in Chania as per her request. He was also waiting for Kevin to let him know when he could take leave from his job as he was still immersed in the current case which seemed to be interminable.

"We better get a move on if we want to get a decent table," announced Kevin arising from the settee and walking to the kitchen to stack the dishwasher with their breakfast things. "It tends to get rather busy there on Sundays," he added.

"Yes, you're right, it does," replied Theo, his reverie now awakened.

He tidied up the papers placing them in the wicker basket to reside in the clot of magazines, Tatler, Country Life, last week's copy of the Times and various Law Society Gazettes. He left Tiddles ensconced on the settee, then strode to the bedroom to select appropriate attire for the gallery.

Chapter Twenty- Two

It was on a Tuesday when cocky expired, his lifeless body lying upside down to be discovered by Theo when he drew off the cover from the cage.

"Kev, oh Kev," Theo yelled from the kitchen.

Kevin came running from the bedroom.

"What? What's happened?"

His eyes navigated to the cage where the lifeless parrot lay.

He put his arm around Theo.

"It was probably for the better, darl," he said.

"We knew he was not having any quality of life."

"Ye, yes I know," sniffed Theo. "But I thought he might pull through with that medication."

Theo had taken it to the vet and had obtained some ointment to apply to the area of his chest which he had been constantly scratching denuding it of feathers. He also was given Prozac in an attempt to relieve cocky's anxiety.

"Maybe it was the Prozac?" queried Theo. "Or that ointment which he would have ingested."

Kevin told Theo that they might never know what caused his demise. He told him that at least now the bird was free from all the stress and suffering and was now at peace with his owner, Albert. He would never tell him that he had given the bird more Prozac than was what was prescribed. He wanted the bird put out of its misery and stop its infernal screeching which had been driving him to distraction. Theo took on board what Kevin was saying and felt comforted by his words but was anxious regarding the bird's disposal as there was no garden in the complex.

He decided that he would place the bird in a shoebox and when it was dark, leave it at the door of the veterinary clinic. Kevin thought that was a good idea. He had visions of Theo wanting to dig up an area in the nearby park which would lead to a fine by the council if he was caught. Theo hurried to the bedroom and opened one of the cupboards in which he found an old shoe box. He opened the cage, tenderly lifted cocky and placed him in the box. He took a piece of paper and wrote, thank you for disposing of our bird. He put the note inside an envelope which he stuck onto the box with sticky tap then placed the box near the front door.

Kevin decided he would like the cage removed before he left for work. He wanted the kitchen restored to its former equanimity and cleanliness as soon as possible. They carried the cage into the lift then placed it outside the building for the council to remove on the next collection day. When they returned to the kitchen, they discovered

Tiddles sniffing around the space where the cage had resided the spilt seeds covering the floor.

"I wonder if puss will miss him?" Theo said sotto voce. Kevin had commenced vacuuming the floor.

"I can do that," said Theo grabbing the vacuum. "You better jump in the shower and go to work."

"Ok, if you don't mind, darl. I didn't realise it was that late."

"We haven't even had breakfast," said Theo.

"I can grab a coffee and danish en route," Kevin replied dashing off to the bathroom.

Theo turned on the vacuum, the noise making Tiddles scuttle out of the room to the refuge of the bed. As Theo suctioned the seeds he thought of poor cocky now with Albert, his loyal owner.

"Bye, pet. See you tonight," said Kevin planting a kiss on Theo's cheek as he dashed out the door briefcase in hand, a slipstream of citrus after- shave in his wake.

"See you, have a good day and don't work too hard," replied Theo who was still concerned about his partner's health. He put away the vacuum then turned on the jug to make tea. While he waited for it to boil, he thought about the list of things he had to do. Firstly, there was a funeral for an elderly lady at 10.30 at Hendon crematorium. It would be another small affair just like all the other aged departed and he wondered if that would be the case for him when his time came, a minute assembly of mourners. The sons of the deceased had advised him that she had a love of knitting spending her time making jumpers and beanies for her sons and grandsons and for the various charitable organisations who would distribute her items to the needy. Her coffin would be adorned with knitting needles, balls of wool and two brightly coloured jumpers. After the funeral, he was going back to his mother's house to meet the removalists who would remove the settee, the nest of tables and the chest of drawers and transport them to the Salvation Army depot. He was not looking forward to that as it would signify an ending, a finality to his former life, the house, just a shell, devoid of its contents. The kettle now boiled, he took down a packet of tea and spooned it into the pot. As he waited for it to brew, he put a piece of raisin toast into the toaster. Tiddles came padding into the room.

"Hey puss," said Theo reaching down to pat him but he wandered off, tail in the air, preferring to sniff around the area where the cage had been.

"You missing poor cocky?" Theo asked as the toast popped up to be buttered.

He poured the tea, the scent of Bergamot rising with the steam, then leaving the cat to its devices, took his breakfast out to the balcony. The sun had just enough warmth for him to feel comfortable, to sit there without a jacket. Summer was around the corner. Summer, his favourite season replete with long sunny days, sandy beaches, picnics and drives into the country. He and Kevin both loved the country especially the areas which also had beaches or lakes. The UK had plenty of those places, some of them more easily accessible to London, only a couple of hours commute on the train.

He took a bite of toast and sipped his tea savouring the flavour his gaze alighting on the collection of pot plants containing a myriad of blooms which were Kevin's pride and joy, his green thumb responsible for the impressive display. Lavender, marigolds, geraniums and pansies all blended together in perfect harmony. His mother had been an avid gardener, out in the yard as much as she could, stabbing the hoe into the earth to extricate the stubborn weeds. Through his child's eyes he wondered why she drove it so forcefully and it was only in these later years he surmised that she was probably venting her anger and frustration because of the state of her life, her marriage and that bastard of a husband. He was grateful his relationship with Kevin had been successful. Naturally, they had their ups and downs like any couple, Kevin's antipathy towards the bird developing into a heated row tinged with sour words and recriminations. He berated himself for adopting the bird in the first place. If he had known it would engender such animosity, he would never have contemplated it. However, their differences had resolved like all the others with goodnight kisses and penitential words. Tiddles came wandering out to sniff around the pansies and avail himself of the sun.

The phone rang.

Theo rose from the table and walked inside to answer it.

"Hello,"

"Hi darl, its me. I have some news."

"Oh, what?"

"Well, you had better be sitting down."

"No, I'm standing here in the hall."

As Kevin's glad tidings echoed through the line, Theo could hardly comprehend what he was hearing. The detective had tracked down Stavros in a care home not far away in Greece, but here in England, in Ealing! My God, he yelled! My dad, he's alive! Although there was no proof and Kevin had advised him not to raise his hopes too much, Theo could not help thinking that Stavros was indeed his father.

They both hung up. Theo returned to the balcony, to the chair he was sitting on when the phone had rang-the tea cold, the cat gone, the morning transformed.

He was somewhat distracted at the funeral nearly forgetting to place the candle near the picture of the deceased, his mind taken up with thoughts of his father. What would he look like? Would he resemble Theo, and more importantly would he be able to converse with him and tell him everything about the relationship he had with his mother? He wanted to go and see him as soon as possible, to go by himself if Kevin did not have time to accompany him.

The funeral concluded with the old favourite hymn, The Lord is my shepherd and Theo wasted no time driving to his mother's house. As he drove, he felt the beginning of a headache. They were not as frequent as before, the injections seeming to alleviate their regularity. The bleeding episodes were also less severe for which he was grateful. He felt inside his pocket for the packet of Tylenol which he always carried. He would take two tablets when he arrived. He switched on the stereo for some uplifting music something to match his jubilant mood. A Beautiful Day by U2 reverberated through the speaker. Oh, yes, it is certainly that, Theo thought as he turned up the volume and sang along uncaring who saw or heard him.

He arrived at the house in good time before the removalists. The first thing he did was swallow the tablets with some water. He had left a glass there for times such as these. Everything else he had taken to the charities or thrown out for the council to collect as was the case with cocky's cage. Poor cocky. He had taken him in the shoebox in the dark of the night to leave it at the veterinary clinic feeling like some sort of burglar stealthily creeping up to the entrance hoping nobody would observe him and thankful that nobody did.

He walked from the kitchen into the sitting room where stood the nest of tables, the china cabinet and the settee. He went to it and sat down thinking of all the times he had sat there with his mother as she read books to him, or they watched television together. They were happy, peaceful times, just the two of them without the malevolent presence of his father.

He thought he would ensure there was nothing left under the cushions, any odd coins or notes which might have slipped down into the spaces. At a funeral one of the assembly had told him that someone had unearthed quite a bit of money in a settee, the owner having hoarded it there for some unknown reason. He pulled off the cushions and placed them on the floor. His hand searched around, deep down into the settee. He felt something hard. It did not feel like money. He wrenched it out and there it was, a book, a diary and it belonged to his darling mother. He grabbed it and held it to his heart. He was in disbelief that after all his searching in cupboards and drawers here it was stuffed into the settee the whole time. Poor mum, she must have forgotten she had left it there. Surely, she would not have done it on purpose for him her son to discover?

A knock at the door.

The removalists lumbered in. Theo stood by and observed meaty arms transporting the items to the van parked outside. Soon he felt as bereft as the room which now echoed with a stillness, a silence, all its contents gone never to return.

He turned his thoughts to the diary and thanked God, he had found it before the removalists arrived. He could hardly wait to read what was written, to discover if it would shed any light on Stavros, her lover. He wanted to know what sort of person he was, if he was kind and caring of his mother, not like that monster she had married. He knew he would feel like a trespasser, an intruder reading his mother's secret and most private thoughts, however, knowing her she would most likely understand and forgive him.

Chapter Twenty-Three

The fog had lifted by the time they approached Brentwood.

"Not much further darl," said Kevin overtaking a utility truck which contained a mattress which looked precariously about to topple off onto the A4.

"Fuck, that's so dangerous," commented Kevin.

"Telling me," Theo replied. "Some people don't have any idea about securing their load."

The episode had been a distraction from Theo's thoughts as up until now his mind had been focussed on their final destination, Ealing, the Acorn Nursing Home where Stavros would be waiting. Stavros, who he now knew was his father as he had read the diary. Theo had spent a sleepless night tossing and turning, his mind mired in worry about the upcoming day. How would he be greeted? Would he be able to talk to him? He knew his mother had loved him her written words attesting to Stavros' kindness and love for her. He had felt like a trespasser reading her private thoughts, the amatory words, some sentences bringing a blush to Theo's cheeks especially the one which stated; "Oh my darling, how I miss tasting your sweet cock." He could not visualise his mother having intercourse with a man let alone indulging in any other sexual activities. He read they had made love in one of the temples of the Acropolis, sneaking out when all was quiet.

He also read about the man she had married, his pseudo father, the details of which had shocked him to the core. Apart from being an abuser, he had been incarcerated for embezzlement, had died not from tuberculosis in a sanitarium, but in jail! She had suspected he might have even murdered some Greek waiter in Brighton! Why did his mother keep this from him all through the years? He could understand not telling him when he was a child but surely, she should have told him when he was adult enough to withstand such news. Kevin had been as taken aback as Theo when he had been apprised of all this. His lover through tears hardly able to enunciate what he had read about that bastard his mother had married. Kevin had put him to bed with brandy and a sleeping pill which he hoped would serve as a bulwark to the shock, a salve for his trauma.

During his reading, he discovered that she had become pregnant to Stavros in Athens, that he had to return to his wife who was running the farm in Perivolaki. Divorce was impossible for him and there was no other option but to leave Meg and resume his marriage. He learnt that his mother also did not have many options available to her, a pregnant woman to be shunned and pilloried by society, a shameful slut of a daughter which her parents, especially her religious mother would have called her, upon her return to London. So, she had seduced and coerced the unsuspecting soldier on the Nea Hellas, had married him there on the high seas, to be a respectable married woman, he unaware of her impregnation by her Greek lover, Stavros.

They drove into Ealing, and on through an insalubrious area, Theo concentrating on locating the correct street.

"It should be the next one on the left, Bardwell Road," said Theo.

Kevin drove on and turned into Bardwell.

"It's number 94," said Theo peering at the numbers of the houses his excitement and apprehension building inside him.

"Here it is," he said.

Kevin slowed down and looked around for a parking space.

"There's one on the other side of the road," enthused Theo.

Kevin drove over and managed to reverse into a rather tight space.

"Well done," said Theo pleased that he had found a park for them without too much hassle as that is what he could do without today. Kevin had a proclivity towards impatience and irritation especially where parking spaces were involved. His mood was also verging on irascibility of which Theo had borne the brunt after he directed Kevin towards a wrong turning leading Kevin to execute a sharp U-turn. It was all the stress he was under at work Theo opined and wished his lover would take steps to address it, to make an appointment with the doctor. The last time he had attended the clinic his blood pressure had been 170 over 90 which was much too high. He was also smoking which did not help matters Theo ensuring he smoked only on the balcony and not inside telling him it would exacerbate Theo's hay fever. He was ambivalent about Kevin coming with him today. On the one hand, he would have preferred a private meeting with Stavros, but he needed Kevin's support as he ventured into this unknown enclave.

They disembarked and Kevin locked the doors. They walked across the road to number 94.

"It looks rather drab," commented Kevin.

"Maybe it's better inside," Theo said hoping he was right as the building they were confronting had seen better days. The paint was peeling from the walls and the A was missing from the sign so it read Corn Care Home instead. Another sign affixed to the fence stated SMOKING PERMITTED, the NO having been scratched out probably by vandals. There was no garden to speak of just a wasteland of stony ground with a few hardy weeds poking through.

They walked through the gate which was off its hinges.

"Well, here goes," said Theo pressing the buzzer.

The door opened.

A skinny woman greeted them.

"Good morning," said Theo.

"We are here to see Mr Stavros Poulos."

"Ok, come in then," said the woman closing the door.

They followed her along a corridor, the worn pitted lino and peeling walls testament to the insalubriousness of the place, past a room filled with what looked to be incontinence pads as the combined smell of disinfectant, urine and cooked cabbage assailed their senses. Replete with disdain, Theo and Kevin exchanged glances. They walked through a room containing brown plastic- coated chairs in which sprawled people in various states of consciousness. A television high on a wall was silent, the pictures distorted as a teletext flashed across the screen.

What sort of place was this? Thought Theo as he cast his eyes on the scene before him, all these poor pathetic people living in a place like this at the end of their lives. This place in which his father resided.

They followed the woman out of the sitting room.

"He's in there," she announced, pointing to a room on the left.

They walked over to a closed door, knocked then entered.

He was sitting in a wheelchair facing the window, his wispy head bowed down as in sleep.

Theo crept over and tenderly placed his hand on his shoulder which alerted Stavros to Theo's presence.

He stirred a little and raised his head.

"Hello," said Theo, not knowing what else to say. He could not say," hello, I am your long -lost son here to see you," which he wanted to say more than anything but knew it to be impossible.

Just when Theo thought Stavros was about to respond a nurse entered the room and ignoring Theo and Kevin walked briskly over to the patient.

"Well, Stav," she said taking his hand to check his pulse." Looks like you have some visitors, isn't that nice?" She dropped his wizened hand and then wrote something on a whiteboard on the wall.

"Excuse me, but could I have word please?" asked Theo beckoning the nurse over away from Stavros.

She approached.

"Sorry for any inconvenience," Theo commenced.

"But would you know the name of the person who answers the phone here?"

"Oh, anyone who is available. Usually, I answer it."

"Oh, ok, good," replied. "Well, do you remember a man, a detective by the name of Nikos speaking to you about Stavros, Mr Poulos."

"Oh, yes, how could I forget that phone call. Are you two something to do with that?"

Then, huddled in the corner of the room, a conversation followed in which they all introduced themselves. Her name was Barbara and she had been astounded to learn that he and Kevin had embarked with the assistance of this detective on a search for this patient, Stavros. A search which had commenced in the wilds of Greece to conclude here in the suburb of Ealing. That a diary had been unearthed proving Stavros was Theo's biological father. It was such an extraordinary event, she had commented, and was worthy of a book. She advised them that Stavros had dementia and was rather deaf so he would be unable to hear what was being said. He also was unable to walk, the wheelchair attesting to his immobility. She had told them that he was a long- term resident, a widower with no other relatives. He had been the owner of a cafe and had been placed into care by a Greek friend who himself had apparently now passed away.

"Meg, Meg," whispered Stavros interrupting their conversation.

Theo and Kevin looked at each other in amazement.

"He always calls me that," said the nurse. "It comes with the dementia, I'm afraid. Lately, it's the only thing he can manage to say."

Theo explained that Meg was his mother's name.

"Oh, well that explains it. He still remembers her. People with this condition retain past memories but have trouble with present ones. Go over and sit with him. I'm sure he would like you to talk to him."

As Kevin lingered in the background with the nurse, Theo returned to Stavros' side. He pulled a chair over and sat down. He took his frail hand.

"Yahsoo," he said" hello," this time in Greek. He had looked up a couple of Greek words which he surmised might be helpful, put him in good stead at a time such as this.

Stavros looked at Theo who noticed that although his eyes were rheumy, they still retained the colour of anthracite, the same colour as Theo's eyes which Kevin always thought. This was indeed what would bind them, thought Theo, we have the same colour eyes. This would be the link to him, his father.

Stavros blinked a couple of times; a questing look on his jowly face. He did not know who this man was. Was he a doctor? He looked too young to be a doctor, the doctor who came to see him was old, with a beard so it could not be him.

"I'm Theo, Stavros," said Theo, his voice trembling, "and over there," he added pointing to Kevin," is my friend, Kevin."

"We have come from London to see you and, if you agree, we will come and visit you again. We might even be able to take you outside for a little walk. Do you think you would like that?"

Stavros nodded his head.

"Ok, that's great then," said Theo.

Barbara and Kevin came over.

"If you like," Barbara suggested hearing what Theo had said, "you could take him for a walk now, before his lunch. He doesn't get out very much as we are always short staffed and too busy."

"Ok, what do you think Kev?" asked Theo.

Kevin looked at his watch and agreed.

Barbara ensured Stavros' blanket was secured over his lap. She manoeuvred the chair from its position near the window and wheeled Stavros out of the room with Theo and Kevin following behind.

She left them in the corridor with instructions to take him to a park which was a couple of blocks down the street.

"When you come out of the gate turn right and keep walking. You can't miss it. It's called Anderson Park. Oh, and I nearly forgot. One of you will need to sign the book over there at reception."

Kevin left Theo with Stavros and went over to a desk where a book lay open. He wrote his name and signed. He rejoined Theo and the two of them pushed the chair through the sitting room passing the same stupefied bodies, the vacant eyes drawn to the flickering TV as the malodorous odours of urine and cabbage followed them through the door.

Chapter Twenty-Four

Stavros was back in his room where he preferred to be, away from the other inmates, the dross of the sitting room, just him and his thoughts. He had enjoyed going to the park with those two fellows especially the one he thought was called Theo who talked to him about all sorts of things, pointing out and naming the various shrubs and flowers growing there. He was fond of placing his hand on his shoulder and ensuring his knees were snug under the blanket. Maybe he was a doctor, a Greek one as Theo was a Greek name. Whoever he was, he certainly was caring! The other fellow did not have much to say. He was always looking at his phone or checking his watch which looked expensive. However, he had bought them all a coffee from the kiosk which was nice and had reminded him of the thick black coffee he and his darling used to make from the brika in Athens. Theo had told him they would visit him again, would even take him to a cafe for lunch. He would look forward to that, to eat something better than fish fingers and wilted lettuce which was what they gave them here in the Home. He had thought it was nice when the two of them had planted kisses on his cheek before they left. He had missed being kissed especially on the lips which led him to wonder when his darling will come. Maybe he mused, we could go to the Acropolis if it's safe, to have a cuddle in our favourite spot in the corner of the temple. But she never wants to go anymore. When I was able to ask her, she would say she is too busy and she will go another day. His mind was always jumbled with an array of thoughts about his life, the war, being nursed by his darling in the cave at Chania and that place at Alexandras Avenue. He recollected the surly countenance of his wife who had ultimately died from an unspecified disease, the farm becoming unsustainable, sold to his neighbour for a pittance. He had packed up then and gone to Athens renting a room in one of the tenements which was listed for demolition. He drove a taxi around the city's unkempt, apres war environs, attempting to assuage all his grief and guilt in bottles of raki and sex with women none of the latter a match for his only true love, Meg. He had managed to save enough money to board a ship as she had done, emigrating to the shores of England, there to sweat and toil in a café in Camden washing a continuous pile of greasy plates and pans trying to earn enough to establish his own café, to be his own boss. It had taken a few years, but his hard work had paid off. With the assistance of his Greek friends, one in particular lending him some money, finally his dream had come to fruition. In a laneway off the high street in Camden, XENOS CAFÉ was open for business.

He had put all his energy into the enterprise initially working seven days a week until he could afford to employ someone to assist him. He was then able to have two days off a week, one day to clean the room above the café where he lived, the other to board a train and take in the sights of the various places in England. He possessed a restlessness, always on the move, trying to escape the pervasive thoughts which haunted him, the war, his failed marriage, the lack of progeny and his one true love, Meg. He always thought of her, her radiant smile, her raven hair, the perfume she wore. The last sighting of her when he had left that fateful morning hovering at the door in her flimsy nightdress a bewildered despairing look painted on her sweet face. It had taken all his courage, his fortitude to leave her, to put one foot in front of the other and return to the farm. He always wondered what had happened to her, did she marry or have children or was she like him condemned to be a wanderer in a dismal desert? He had visions of the hospital where he had been placed after collapsing on the grease spattered floor behind the counter, one of his customers coming to his aid before summoning an ambulance. That was the beginning of his declining health, a stroke then the onset of dementia and here he was, a frail immobile old man joined with the other unfortunates, the detritus of society.

As Stavros sat mired in his thoughts, Theo and Kevin were discussing the parlous state of the care home where Theo's father was incarcerated. They were both in disbelief that aged people who had contributed to society, going to war and being wounded as Stavros did, could be treated in such a fashion.

"By the state of them, I'm sure they were all drugged," commented Theo as he finished off the glass of red wine and then poured himself another.

"Yes, I was thinking the same. It would be less work for the staff if they are all sedated. God forbid we ever end up like that, I would prefer to be shot," replied Kevin.

"God, yes. And the smell of the place. It would turn your stomach."

"Do you think we could try and get him out of there?"

"What, you mean move him into another facility?"

"No, I was thinking of having him stay here with us."

"What? Here?"

"Why not. There's room."

"But who's going to look after him? We can't."

"I thought we could employ a nurse."

"A live-in nurse?"

"No, someone who comes in on a daily basis."

Kevin thought Stavros would be better off in a more decent facility, maybe somewhere closer to them in London. He did not like the idea of having him here living with them in close proximity and with some strange nurse popping in and out at all hours. It would totally disrupt their living arrangements. He also posited the cost of the enterprise which Theo countered by saying he would fund it from the proceeds of the sale of his mother's estate. There was already a good offer for the house which he thought he would accept.

"Please, Kev," Theo begged with tears welling. "It would mean so much if I could spend with him what remaining time he has which by the look of him probably will not be long."

"Let me think a bit more about it," Kevin offered, popping an olive into his mouth. "We have only just met the poor sod. At least give him time to become used to us otherwise he might think we are abducting him."

Kevin's words gave Theo some solace and he hoped and prayed he would come around to his way of thinking. Surely, he could see that now he had found his father he needed to try and spend as much time as possible to make up for all the years they had spent apart. How wonderful it would be to have him here in the same house, to bestow care and affection on him. In a beautiful environment devoid of malodorous smells, of insensible people and inedible food. He envisioned taking him for walks along the river, stopping at cafes for coffee. He seemed to enjoy going to the park with them and drinking the coffee Kevin had bought. It took a bit of effort to understand what type of coffee he wanted, Kevin showing him the menu, pointing out espresso, cappuccino and flat white, Stavros settling on espresso. Theo wished he was able to communicate as the only word he had uttered was the name of his dear mother. Maybe when he was here in a more caring environment, his speech would improve. Oh, God, how I wish I could say, "Dad, I am your son, Theo," but even if he did, he probably would be unable to understand.

Chapter Twenty-Five

Theo had bought a sofa bed for his father to sleep and moved it into the sitting room. He had hung a picture of Santorini which he surmised would make him feel more at home. Kevin had relented. After more pleading and a contretemps which had developed into a full- blown argument where words were uttered then regretted, words about Kevin allowing Theo to adopt," that bloody cockatoo", about the mess and the noise it had made and "it was a good thing that it had expired." That statement had greatly perturbed Theo leading him to suffer a migraine preventing him from officiating at a wedding and locating someone else to take his place. Noticing how his cutting words had affected him, Kevin had apologised blaming the stress of work and the upcoming court case. He had tried to make amends by placing a cool washer on Theo's forehead and drawing the blinds against the light with a promise of allowing Stavros to stay on the condition that a nurse would be engaged to care for him. That had been what Theo had been praying and hoping for, his father would see out his remaining days here with them. The care home had been advised and, in the following weeks, Theo had driven to Ealing whenever he was free to take his father out to lunch or walks around the suburb. Always cognisant of his father's nationality, one day he had sourced a Greek restaurant, The Athenian, the only one in Ealing. Decorated with fishing nets strung across the ceiling and music from Zorba the Greek the place was devoid of customers. Theo thought it was a bad sign, the food would be inedible, and he was regretting taking his father there.

As soon as they had entered, a rotund waiter pounced flourishing a large comprehensive menu at Theo while reeling off the specials of the day as he led them to a table in a dark corner. "Could we please sit over there, near the window?" Theo asked, thinking that they could have their choice of tables as they were presently the only customers. "Ok, as you like," said the waiter. Theo wheeled the chair over and manoeuvred it into position. He sat down and perused the menu as the waiter hovered alongside. Theo asked Stavros would he like some calamari, or maybe some moussaka? Stavros nodded. Theo ordered the two dishes. He thought if they could not consume it all, the leftovers could be taken with them. He could take some and Stavros could have his later for his dinner instead of some stale sandwich. He then ordered two glasses of red wine as the care home said that Stavros was permitted to have a glass now and then if he wished.

Theo found it hard communicating with him, his deafness and the music cancelling out much conversation. Theo had resorted to painting a smile on his face and patting his father's hand. His heart had been warmed when he had responded, a little smile indicating he was enjoying being here having lunch with him at this Greek establishment.

The calamari arrived first, a large plate garnished with slices of lemon.

"Ah, thank you," said Theo. "Or, should I say efharisto?"

The waiter bowed and disappeared into the nether regions of the kitchen.

Theo put some calamari on Stavros' plate and squeezed over some lemon.

Stavros stabbed a piece and popped it into his mouth.

"It's good?" asked Theo looking at his father.

There was no reply instead he started contorting in his chair, trying to cough, his face stricken with panic.

"Oh, no, oh my God, are you alright, are you choking?" yelled Theo as he leapt from his chair.

"Hello, help, help please, someone, my father is choking."

Two waiters alerted to Theo's cries came running out from the kitchen.

They hauled Stavros from his wheelchair and roughly put him on another chair. The fat waiter then started banging his back until there was a strangled cough and the piece of calamari shot out of his mouth onto the floor.

"Oh, God, oh thank heavens you are ok," Theo said as he wiped Stavros' face with a napkin.

"Thank you both so much," he said to the waiters. "You probably saved his life."

"Ok, we glad to help," said the fat waiter pleased that he was able to assist. It had been somewhat of a diversion from an otherwise tedious day.

The three of them returned Stavros to his wheelchair, the colour now returning to his face.

After that incident, the life and death drama, Theo was worried about Stavros eating any more food. He did not want him to die here in this restaurant. Why did he bring him here in the first place? He should have known it would not be a normal lunch such as what he has with Kevin. His poor father was frail and probably unused to swallowing such things as fried fish. Was it any wonder he nearly choked? He is my responsibility, and he could have died here at this table in this restaurant.

He looked across at Stavros now reaching for his wine. Theo leapt up and taking the glass from his hand gave him small sips.

"There, easy does it," said Theo. "You gave me such a fright you know."

Stavros' expression was rather blank, and he reached again for another piece of calamari.

"Better not eat any more of those," Theo advised. "We will wait for the moussaka. At least it will be soft."

Up until he choked, Stavros had been enjoying himself. He liked this place, the music, reminding him of happier times, dancing with his friends like whirling dervishes, when life was sweet, before he took his marital vows. Was he in Greece, on one of the islands? He did not know. This man Theo was nice, taking me here and other places. Did he say that I was going to stay with him for awhile in London? I thought I heard him calling me his father. That cannot be right. I never had any children. Maybe Meg will be coming. I'm glad she did not see me choking, she would be as worried as this Theo. Sometimes I have trouble swallowing. The nurse said I would have to eat pureed food if it continues. His mind wandered around the time of his childhood, the unheated house, the brass candle burners hanging from nails on the walls, the handmade wicks burning in olive oil. The old donkey which his father would load with fresh water, wine, bread and tomatoes to take down the perilous track to the beach where they would extinguish their cares in the azure water. Then he was seeing all those nun's skulls in the convent and how terrified he had been.

The moussaka arrived and Theo cut off a tiny portion and fed it to his father.

"Make sure you chew it well," he instructed, thinking his father was similar to a child and he the father, not the other way around.

Theo ate a few more of the calamari which were by now rather cold. He thought of the calamari he had eaten at that café in Chania with his mother, the place where they fed the blind cat. Beautiful Chania, the place where mum and his father first met, his father now seated beside him, an old frail man, choking on food, his youth and virility dissolved into the mist of time. It will happen to me and to Kevin, we will also grow old and frail. We must make the most of what time we are allocated on this earth, to treasure every moment like it was our last and not indulge in petty arguments.

He fed Stavros another piece of moussaka which thank goodness, he swallowed without any mishap. He reached for the glass, Theo allowing him to drink some by himself thinking surely, he would not choke on wine. He hoped he had not heard him calling him father, he had not meant to utter the word in his presence, but the shock of his choking had seen to that.

They ate as much as they could Theo requesting a doggie bag for the leftovers then rang the taxi to collect them. He was presented with the bill which he paid with his Amex card adding a substantial tip to the total for the saving of his father's life.

"I cannot thank you enough, and so sorry for any inconvenience," said Theo as he took the receipt. "And" he added, "I will recommend your restaurant to all my friends." The food had indeed been good, his earlier doubts unfounded.

"Thank you," said the waiter bowing. He ran over to hold open the door. Theo pushed Stavros out to the street where the wheelchair accessible taxi waited to escort them back to the home.

Chapter Twenty-Six

The rosewood coffin bedecked with white lilies stood at the front of the chapel, the same chapel in which Theo's mother had been farewelled. Amongst the flowers nestled the dog tag belonging to the fallen soldier, Stavros, lover of Meg, father of Theo.

The call had come in the early hours of the morning, the time when usually all bad news worms its way into the ears of the receiver. The nurse, Barbara had told Theo that Stavros had fallen out of bed, hitting his head and, despite all efforts by the staff, had never regained consciousness.

Theo could hardly comprehend was he was being told, his father who he was just getting to know, who was going to come here to live with them, to be cared for and showered with affection was dead. Kevin had taken the phone from him to thank Barbara for delivering the message. He had then cradled Theo in his arms trying to soothe him with words of comfort as Theo cried as though his heart would break.

"At least you were able to spend some time with him, darl," said Kevin.

Theo's tear- stained face looked at Kevin.

"Yes, I suppose I should be grateful for that, especially when I took him to that Greek restaurant. In his own way, I think he enjoyed it."

"What, the one where he nearly choked?"

"Yes, that one."

"Well, only for the quick thinking of those waiters he might have expired there and then."

As the first light of dawn stole into the room, they sat on the bed and talked about how fortuitous it was that they had been able to locate him after all these years. How he had lived to a grand old age. How lucky Theo had been to discover his mother's diary revealing how kind and caring Stavros had been to her. That the two of them now were reunited in everlasting love. This had brought a fresh flow of tears as Theo thought of his mother and father clasped together in God's holy light.

Theo said, his voice shaky, "I wish I could have told him that I was his son and I loved him, but now it's too late."

Kevin took hold of his hand.

"I know, darl but in his condition, he would not have understood or probably not believed you. You know how he used to think Barbara was your mum."

"Don't beat yourself up about it, just be grateful you found him and cared for him in the remaining time he had."

That was what Theo had to tell himself, what he had to cling to. He had been given the chance to reconnect with his dad before he died which could have well been years before Theo had known he existed.

The paperwork had been signed and arrangements made for the funeral and cremation, now here they were, assembled in the chapel, the undertaker, Nick, the detective, a few close friends, Kevin and himself.

The hymn, Morning Has Broken had ended. It was time for Theo to arise, to take his place at the podium where he had stood for his darling mother's funeral, to say a few words in honour of this man, his dear departed father. He cleared his throat then related what had been a love story. Stavros had met his soul mate, his nurse, my mother Meg during the war, caring for his wounds in a hospital cave in Chania. Their love had produced me, Theo, for I was his son. He told them about his loyalty to his wife, to return to her and the farm in Perivolaki in Greece not knowing that Meg was pregnant with his child when he left her in Athens. He had emigrated here to England where he established his Greek café in Camden. The attendees heard that Theo had discovered his mother's diary, along with the dog tag which Stavros had left in the tenement in Athens, which tag is now proudly displayed. Here, Theo pointed to the coffin so everyone could see it nestled among the flowers. They heard about Nick, the private detective who, after a lot of searching, had tracked down Stavros in the care home in Ealing.

He finished the eulogy with a poem which he deemed appropriate, dedicated to a soldier by Sir Walter Scott however, with a couple of minor alterations:

Dear dad rest! Your warfare's over
Sleep the sleep that knows not breaking
Dream of battled fields no more
Days of danger, nights of waking
In our isle's enchanted hall
Hands unseen your couch are strewing
Fairy strains of music fall
Every sense in slumber dewing
Dear dad, rest! Your warfare's over
Dream of fighting fields no more
Sleep the sleep that knows no more
Sleep the sleep that knows not breaking
Morn of toil, nor night of waking.

He walked down from the podium relieved that he had not become a quivering mess, he had been able to recount and say what he wanted to say, to let people know about his father's life and to proudly profess in public that he had indeed been his father's son. As he slid into the seat, Kevin gave his hand a squeeze and from the corner of his eye he detected Barbara was giving him a thumbs up sign.

Chapter Twenty-Seven

Theo and Kevin were in Chania at the same restaurant and even the same table where Theo and his mother had dined, the precious cargo at their feet. They had traversed the same cobblestoned path, on down to the roiling sea and past the café of the blind cat where Theo and Meg had fed it the sardines.

Kevin had taken his overdue leave and was in the process of evaluating his stressful lifestyle. He had taken Theo's advice and consulted a doctor who had warned that he was a candidate for a heart attack if he did not take steps to ameliorate the situation. Theo also was assessing his situation. After the deaths of his mother and father he was finding it difficult to officiate at funerals with all the sadness they entailed. The last funeral was for a child who had been killed by a hit and run driver.

"Cheers," said Theo clinking his glass of Moet with Kevin's. They surmised it was what the occasion warranted, something fizzy and celebratory.

"To your mum and dad," replied Kevin.

"Yes, indeed, to them."

Kevin sat back seemingly mesmerised by the scene before him.

"Beautiful? Isn't it Kev?"

"It's certainly spectacular, darl and even better than you described."

The ancient venetian lighthouse was before them, the waves pounding its base as the sky signalled the onset of sunset, emitting a golden hue. The strains of Verdi adding to the ambience.

"I'm so glad you were able to take leave, Kev and come with me."

"I always planned to come; you know that pet. It's just that it took a bit longer than I thought. It's been a good holiday, hasn't it?"

Prior to coming to Chania, they had visited Athens seeing all the usual sites, the Acropolis, the Parthenon, the Panathenaic stadium. It was at the Acropolis, in one of the temples that Theo took time looking around to ponder if it was the one where his mum and dad had made love as she had written in her diary. "Do you think it was this one, Kev?" he had asked. "Could be, pet. I guess we will never know. There are a few of them here."

Theo wanted to believe that it was this one in which they were standing. He seemed to have some sort of psychic feeling but maybe it was all wishful thinking. Wherever it was, at least he was here in this ancient monument, here where his mother and father's passion had been spent.

They had gone on to Heraklion staying at a magnificent resort by the beach one morning throwing caution to the wind, both diving into the surf to be immediately wiped out by a rogue wave. They had both struggled out crawling their way over the rough stones to the safety of the beach. "Ha, ha, we made it," laughed Theo. "God, I thought I was done for. It came out of nowhere," replied Kevin trying to get his breath back. "It's probably why we were the only idiots to venture in. There's nobody else here," Theo said shaking the water out of his ear.

"Yes, talk about mad dogs and Englishmen!" They both laughed then collapsed on the sand both content to lay there and listen to the rumbling of the waves hitting the shore until Kevin inched over, put his arm around Theo and placed a kiss on his salty lips. Theo responded hoping that nobody would suddenly appear as he wanted to do more than kiss. However, Kevin withdrew saying that they should complete their amative activity when they were safely ensconced back in their room away from any prying eyes. Good old Kevin, always the sensible one, thought Theo. Unlike me, always rushing in where angels fear to tread. He was so appreciative for Kevin's support, helping him to locate Stavros and agreeing to his living with them which had meant much more than his words could convey.

They had gone to Agia Pelagia on a coach which wound down and down a circuitous road until it reached the secluded beach. Leaving Kevin to relax on a sunlounge, Theo had hired a snorkel so he could observe whatever lurked under the surface, the silvery fish and maybe, if he was fortunate a piece of archaeology lying on the bottom. He had a penchant for such things, something old from the past, various stones or pebbles making their way onto his person. He had pulled a loose stone from a wall in Knossos Palace when Kevin was not looking as he knew he would admonish him for taking it. Kevin had watched Theo dive into the water and float around, his snorkel bobbing about. He waved to Kevin who waved back pleased that his lover was enjoying himself. He knew how much he loved the beach which stemmed from when he was a child. He had told Kevin all about those days at Chalkwell with his mother, the train ride there, his anticipation at arriving with his bucket and spade. Poor Theo, he had thought, he has certainly had a lot to cope with, his young life tainted with the trauma of the man his mother married. At least she had been caring and nurturing, trying to shield him from the worst of it. Kevin would never tell him about the episode with the cockatoo, how he administered the overdose which had killed it. He still felt guilty but, at the time, the bird had been driving him mad with its infernal screeching to say nothing of the skin he kept pecking at leaving it a bleeding pulpy mess. Surely, he had done it a favour and put it out of its misery. At least he had managed to secure Nick, the detective who had tracked down his father, maybe that would compensate for what he had done to the bird.

Theo had emerged from the sea holding aloft some sort of shard. “Look what I found,” he said approaching Kevin proudly showing him his treasure which he handed to him. “What is it?” Kevin asked, feeling and perusing it.

“It could be something Roman. See, there are three letters, ENE inscribed which look to be Latin.”

Kevin looked more closely letting Theo think that he had some actual Roman artifact in his possession and not from some modern building construction.

“Well, it could be darl,” he offered, adding, “the Romans were once all around this area.”

“I know. What luck?” Theo enthused taking his treasure from Kevin and placing it into his backpack. It had been a glorious day, the crystalline water, the jagged cliffs above them over which seagulls swooped and dived. They had taken a walk along the beach to an ancient chapel, so tiny it only permitted one person to enter and stoop down bending their head to avoid a collision with the roof. Kevin allowed Theo to enter first and then it was his turn. He noticed Theo had lit a fresh candle probably in memory of his mother and Stavros. Kevin did not possess the faith which Theo had, his belief in a benevolent God, some fellow with a beard who would take the deceased into his loving arms to live forever with him. His belief was that when you died there was no so- called afterlife, no meeting with your deceased relatives, there was just a black void. He had had a few debates with Theo about the subject, they both concluding to agree to disagree, Theo never wanting to engage in anything which might develop into some sort of fracas.

The waiter glided over with their entrees, oysters natural for Theo and steak tartare for Kevin.

"We should be eating something Greek," commented Kevin as he broke his bread roll in half.

"I think we have had our fill of Grecian cuisine by now, especially what you made for the gathering."

Kevin had put his culinary skills to use for Stavros' wake which had been at their apartment. He had made Greek salads, moussaka and a slow cooked lemon garlic lamb all washed down with bottles of Raki with which Stavros had been toasted, Nick commenting that Kevin should be a chef not a lawyer.

The sky now was tinged with pink and coral, as their main courses duly arrived; rare fillet steaks, one with peppercorn sauce, the other bearnaise. Their conversation revolved around their Grecian holiday which had exceeded all expectations, both resolving to have more like it, to enjoy life while they were able. The proceeds from the sale of Meg's house would go a long way in financing such ventures, they having both decided to decrease the stress in their lives.

Coffee and amaretto had been consumed and the bill paid.

"Ready?" said Kevin observing the sky, which was turning another shade of pink, the golden orb now disappearing from the horizon.

Theo nodded.

They reached down under the table, and each took an urn.

Clasping the containers to their chests, in companionable silence, they walked from the restaurant, past the ancient fortress and on up to the breakwater. On they went until they arrived at the end, the perfect location. Before them stood the magnificent lighthouse silhouetted against the backdrop of the magenta hues of the sky lending a mysterious yet peaceful air to the scene. Theo thought how entranced his mother had been with the beauty of the place, this place called Chania. He thought of the caves not far from here, where the German bombs rained down into the harbour as she tended the wounded soldiers, one who would eventually become his dear father, Stavros.

"You ok?" queried Kevin.

"Yes, I'm good."

They both unscrewed the lids and tipped over the urns watching as the grey dust was carried away on the roil of the sea.

"Bye mum, bye dad. Now you are together," whispered Theo, his face awash with tears.

Kevin put his arm around his lover offering him comfort. He took a tissue and wiped his face. Arm in arm they walked back the way they had come, along the breakwater, past the fortress, up the cobblestoned path and on to weave another design in their own unique tapestry of life.

EPILOGUE

Kevin and Theo relocated to the beautiful village of Grasmere in the lake district purchasing a guest house to which their friends and others would motor from London always keen for a weekend get-away, to partake of Kevin's culinary prowess and enjoy his signature dinner dish of Lakeland stew with black pudding. After his client won the current defamation case, the Judge awarding him the princely sum of 1.4 million pounds, Kevin had stunned the firm by tendering his resignation, his reason being that his health was more important than accruing billable hours and more stress. He had sold the flat in London and, with the proceeds from the sale of Meg's house, they had been able to purchase the house nestled at the foot of the spectacular fells and the lake. Theo had been chuffed to learn that the area had a connection to Wordsworth whose poem he had used at his mother's funeral. Theo had been rather taken aback when his lover suggested they would be running a guest house but he knew Kevin would make a go of it. He was rather a bon vivant and a terrific cook and Theo had every faith their venture would be successful. It had been fortunate that the house was already established as a bed and breakfast and had a regular clientele.

They now owned a dog, a little Cavalier King Charles spaniel called of course, Charlie. He had been initially rebuffed by Tiddles who had swiped the interloper with his paw a couple of times until he decided it was better to live with him in harmony. On their free days, Kevin and Theo would take Charlie for walks around the fells and to the lake breathing in the fresh clear air, Kevin thinking that it was much better than jogging in London's car fumed pollution. His health had markedly improved by the change of lifestyle, his blood pressure dropping to normal levels while Theo's disease had subsided to a more tolerable condition.

Theo had eschewed funerals with all the poignancy they entailed. He was now fully involved with the happiness of weddings some of which were conducted outside in the pretty cottage garden if the weather was sunny or cosily in the dining room before a hearty log fire.

Kevin, not wanting to totally abandon the law, offered his services twice a week at the community centre in the village advising the farmers and anyone else who needed assistance with their legal rights.

In years to come when the Government legislated same sex marriage, Kevin and Theo would become betrothed, Theo specialising in marrying other couples like them, in love and wanting a formal commitment to their relationship.

They would travel to Italy and behold the wonders of Rome and Florence and the beauteous village of Portovenere where their hotel accommodation was in a 12th century fort. The reception/bar, accessed by three flights of steep steps, was filled with dusty ancient bottles of liquor which Theo and Kevin thought had probably been unopened since the start of the Second World War.

To Kevin's call of "buongiorno", the proprietor, an ancient non- English- speaking Italian had manifested from the depths. Surveying the luggage, he had bellowed at the top of his lungs, "Igor!" A few minutes later, from the gloom slouched a miserly creature whose crestfallen countenance signified some class of dogsbody, a hound beaten to submission. He lifted one of the suitcases commenting surprisingly in good English how heavy it was. Feeling sorry for the poor creature, Kevin offered to carry it for him leaving him with the lighter one. With the bag barking at his shins, they followed this Igor up more steps to their room at the top of the edifice.

"Well, it certainly has character," commented Theo, placing his backpack on the bed after Igor had dropped the bag and scuttled away down the steps. They looked around the room which contained a small double bed, a bedside table and a wardrobe. Kevin poked his head into the miniscule bathroom enabling only one person at a time to enter. "Not much room to swing a cat in there," commented

Theo. He came over and joined Kevin on the bed who had been testing its softness. "What about that Igor fellow?" said Kevin. "I know," replied Theo. "I thought he would expire then and there when he lifted the bag," adding, " I don't know how he gets on with other punters' bags, maybe that's why he looks the way he does, beaten down with the effort of it all. And, what about his expression? Talk about hang-dog! Don't think he's cracked a smile for years!" They had a laugh about the whole situation, about the old proprietor, the dusty bar into which nobody entered, the hard done by Igor who from the open door they now observed was hanging out sheets on a line. "No rest for Igor," commented Theo.

What their room lacked made up in character as they both loved the idea of staying in such an ancient site which they discovered was built circa 1200. It was also in a great location, the cafes and restaurants lying at the foot of their building while the view of the sea from their courtyard was spectacular. In those few days spent in Portovenere, they were both enveloped in its charm and history, the ruins of Doria Castle overlooking the beautiful Bay of Poets in which Byron had swum, St Pietro's Church jutting out on the peninsula, the narrow cobblestoned alleys filled with tiny shops and restaurants one of which served the most delicious porcini mushroom pasta. Over that, their final dinner, they both decided they would certainly return to this most wondrous place, the jewel in the crown of cinque terre. The next morning, they bid farewell to the woebegone Igor who seemed glad not to have to assist with carrying their luggage down all those flights of steps. A taxi drove them to the airport and on to Florence where they joined the madding crowds of tourists attempting to enter the Duomo. Both averse to queueing, they instead decided to see the statue of David and the San Lorenzo Church housing the crypt of the Medicis. “I didn’t know he would be that enormous!” said Theo as they sat in an alfresco café sharing a pizza and glasses of Limonata. “What, his dick?” answered Kevin retrieving a piece of mozzarella which was trailing from his mouth. “Ha, ha, no, you joker, I meant the statue.”

“Yes, I thought it would be smaller too. “And, to think he made it out of one piece of marble with no room for mistakes. And then he went on to paint the Sistine Chapel!”

“As you do!” laughed Theo.

They enjoyed their time in Florence, absorbing the culture, walking the length and breadth of the city, over the bridges and indulging in wild boar pasta and coconut gelato topped with dollops of whipped cream, purchasing Florentine soap and a denim cap for Theo which Kevin encouraged, Theo dubious about it suiting his big head. There had been nary a disagreement between them. However, that had not been the case on Lake Como where, in the village of Bellagio, some unsavoury words were traded between the two. They had been on a tour from Milan to Lake Como which would conclude in Lucerne in Switzerland. They had boarded the ferry at Como and had enjoyed their time aboard, taking photos of the tiny villages and even spying the villa in which resided George Clooney. It was when they arrived at Bellagio things took a turn for the worst. Through their ear pods the guide had told the group that after lunch they would meet at the Metropole Hotel from whence they would continue on their way to Switzerland.

"Come on," shouted Kevin pulling the pod from his ear and charging towards a vine covered alfresco restaurant, Theo hot on his heels. "This place looks nice, and it is near the hotel where we have to meet," announced Kevin. They were conducted to a table under an umbrella as menus were flourished at them. "I think I might have heard that guide say something else," commented Theo as he settled on the chair.

"He said to meet at the Metropole Hotel which is just over there," replied Kevin pointing in the direction, seemingly dismissing Theo's comment.

"Now, what do you feel like eating?" he asked.

Theo perused the menu. "What about sharing that seafood pizza and I wouldn't say no to a glass of red?"

"Ok, sounds good." He summoned over one of the waiters who took their order for the wine which was promptly delivered.

"Could we order por favor?" asked Kevin to which the waiter replied he would contact his colleague.

They clinked glasses and observed the other diners wondering if they like them were also on a tour however, judging by their fine and bejewelled clothing, they were probably the affluent locals of Clooney's ilk partaking of their usual alfresco lunch in this beautiful village.

After Kevin had tried to summon a waiter, again being told that a colleague would be contacted, someone finally condescended to take their order.

"What's that about contacting the colleague?" "Talk about ridiculous!" Kevin expostulated. "We could be here all day waiting for our food!"

However, the pizza had been worth waiting for and they had devoured it with relish. Conscious of the time, Theo made his way to the bathroom leaving Kevin to finish his cappuccino.

"We have enough time to go up those steps and take a few photos," said Kevin as he signed the check and put away his credit card.

Bellagio was noted for the numerous steps which ascended and descended through the narrow alleyways which were filled with various boutiques.

"Let's go up here," said Theo

Kevin followed him up the steps which ended at a flower bedecked courtyard with a fountain in the centre. They stood in front of the fountain and took a few selfies.

"We had better get back," said Theo consulting his watch which said 1.50. The time for the tour to meet was 2.00pm.

"Ok, let's go," said Kevin. They sprinted down the steps arriving at the hotel five minutes early and then the time continued with nobody from the tour in sight.

"Where is everyone?" said Theo. "It's already 2.15 and no one is here."

They went over to the ferry wharf where milling crowds were embarking and disembarking from the ferries, but their tour group and their guide were nowhere to be seen. They walked back to the hotel and walked around the surrounding area then returned to the wharf all to no avail.

Kevin took his phone and rang the tour company to ascertain the whereabouts of the group but without success. Theo could sense panic arising in his loins. Where the hell was the group?

"Looks like they went without us," announced Kevin.

"What, went without us? Fuck, Kev. How could they do that, abandoning us here? How the hell are we going to get back?" Theo was envisioning spending thousands of euros for someone to take them back to Milan, hiring a private boat or some such thing.

"I bet that guide said something more which we didn't hear as you were too quick to take off for lunch. We should have waited a bit longer," said Theo his anxiety threatening to undo him.

"Well, don't blame me. You also ran off to that restaurant pretty damn fast. And, will you stop bloody panicking? You're like an old fucking woman," shouted Kevin.

Theo hated the way Kevin was shouting and berating him like he was a little boy. It reminded him of his father. He then thought they would have to spend the night here and what would be the cost of that in this place of high affluence?

While Theo was consumed by his thoughts, Kevin was looking trying to see something which would take them out of this predicament. In the distance, away from the wharf, he noticed what looked like a bus stop.

"Come on."

"Where we going?"

"To what I hope is a bus stop."

Theo scooted after Kevin praying that there would be a bus which would evacuate them.

They arrived to find a few people milling around at what was indeed a bus stop and after Kevin asked someone, discovered that a bus would be arriving in twenty minutes going directly to Como.

"Oh, thank God," said Theo as he collapsed onto the seat his anxiety now dissipating like melting snow.

Kevin sat beside him. "There should be a train we can take from Como to Milan."

"Sorry I snapped at you back there," Kevin added squeezing Theo's hand.

"That's ok, I suppose we were both to blame."

"But I still think it was beyond the pale to abandon us like that. The guy should have taken a head count making sure everyone was accounted for."

"That's right," replied Theo. "Something could have happened to us. We could have had an accident."

Said Kevin, "when we get home, I will contact that company and give them a piece of my mind. We might even be able to receive some class of refund for missing out on Switzerland although, I wouldn't hold my breath."

"No, I wouldn't be counting on getting anything from them. It probably happens all the time on these tours. Some of these Italians can be a bit manyana."

That summoned a laugh as a bus miraculously appeared around the corner. They boarded and secured two seats up the back amazed that the driver did not request any money from them. They both thought it was compensation for being abandoned and missing out on seeing Lucerne and they had paid their city taxes at the hotels which were not cheap.

The trip turned out better than expected. Apart from not having to pay anything, the bus was air conditioned and from their seat their view of the lake and the villages was even more spectacular than when they were aboard the ferry. They looked down upon a huge waterfall cascading over the cliff and were afforded peeks at the gardens of the villas which could not be seen from the ferry. After one hour they arrived in Como just in time to enjoy a gelato before boarding a train to Milan.

"I think everything turned out alright for us in the end even if we didn't get to see Switzerland," said Theo. They were dining at a restaurant in the magnificence of the

Galleria after admiring the splendour of the Milan Cathedral outside.

“Yes, you’re right about that,” replied Kevin. We would not have had time to see this place as the tour would have ended too late. We would have probably gone straight back to the hotel with a takeaway sandwich.”

“It’s what they say, every cloud has a silver lining,” commented Theo as he sliced a piece of the veal schnitzel and popped it into his mouth.

On the final leg of their holiday, they returned to Greece, making their way to the little village of Perivolaki. After making enquiries of the locals, they eventually located the old derelict farm, overgrown with gorse and other plants. Adding to the abject scene, the dilapidated cheese shed leaned drunkenly, ready to topple over with the next gust of wind. A lone goat appeared and commenced munching on the omnipresent weeds stopping every now and then to peer at the two men who had invaded its territory. It was not to know that one of these men was the son of the owner of this abandoned place who was paying his respects to him, Stavos, the father who had never known that he had a son, no longer a child, but now a married middle- aged man called Theo.

About the Author

From an early age, Annette was encouraged to write and was awarded several prizes for English.

A native of Sydney, Australia, she published a short story at the age of twelve. She remained passionate about her writing, but the demands of raising a family left no time for writing.

Now retired, Annette has reignited her passion and has written seven books.

Her interest lies in novels set around the periods of the First and Second World Wars.

Annette lives with her partner, Stephen, at Neutral Bay, a suburb on Sydney harbor in Australia. She has two sons, Mark and Brett, two grandsons, Jaime and Flynn, and a sister, Maree.

Sunset over Chania is her eighth published novel.

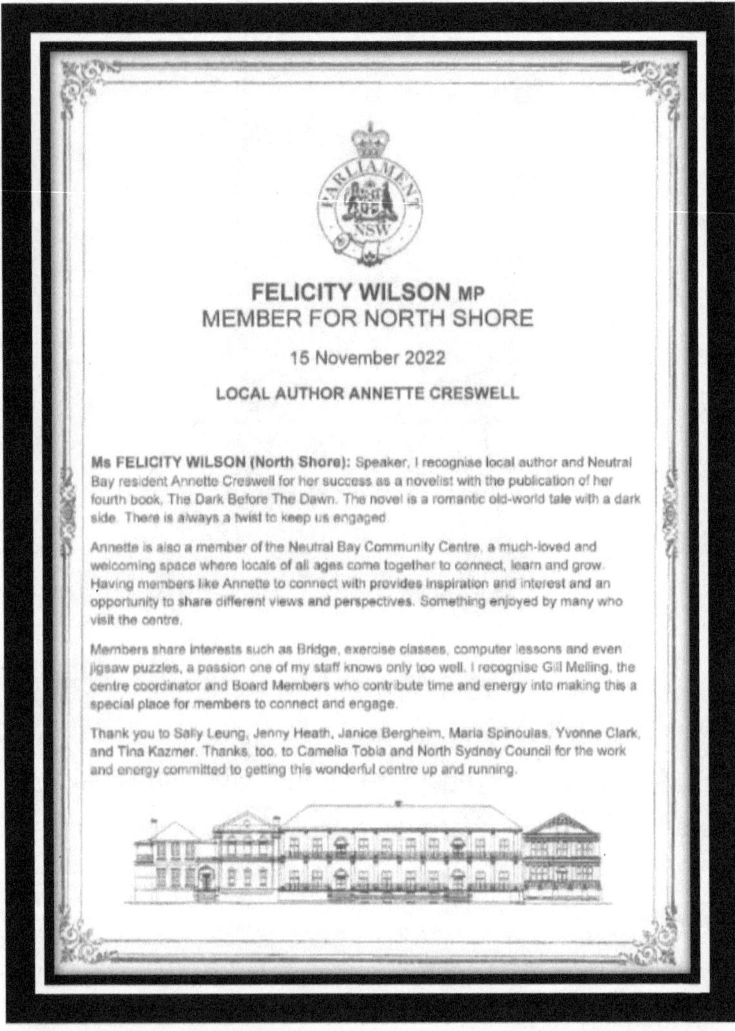

PARLIAMENT NSW

FELICITY WILSON MP
MEMBER FOR NORTH SHORE

15 November 2022

LOCAL AUTHOR ANNETTE CRESWELL

Ms FELICITY WILSON (North Shore): Speaker, I recognise local author and Neutral Bay resident Annette Creswell for her success as a novelist with the publication of her fourth book, The Dark Before The Dawn. The novel is a romantic old-world tale with a dark side. There is always a twist to keep us engaged.

Annette is also a member of the Neutral Bay Community Centre, a much-loved and welcoming space where locals of all ages come together to connect, learn and grow. Having members like Annette to connect with provides inspiration and interest and an opportunity to share different views and perspectives. Something enjoyed by many who visit the centre.

Members share interests such as Bridge, exercise classes, computer lessons and even jigsaw puzzles, a passion one of my staff knows only too well. I recognise Gill Melling, the centre coordinator and Board Members who contribute time and energy into making this a special place for members to connect and engage.

Thank you to Sally Leung, Jenny Heath, Janice Bergheim, Maria Spinoulas, Yvonne Clark, and Tina Kazmer. Thanks, too, to Camelia Tobia and North Sydney Council for the work and energy committed to getting this wonderful centre up and running.

Annette Creswell has also been recognized as an official novelist by the New South Wales Parliament in her community in Neutral Bay, Australia.

www.ingramcontent.com/pod-product-compliance
Lightning Source LLC
LaVergne TN
LVHW090513110826
845146LV00003B/845

* 9 7 9 8 9 9 0 7 0 9 3 4 8 *